"You must be joking!"

"The results plainly show...."

"Stuff and nonsense!" Samantha exclaimed. "The whole idea is so ludicrous."

"Nevertheless, you *are* pregnant," the doctor continued in a firm but gentle voice. "You *are* expecting a baby...a January baby. That's nice."

"*Nice...?*" Samantha gasped. It wasn't that she didn't want a baby. It was just...well, she hadn't even gotten around to thinking about marriage, children and all that stuff. That was part of life which, up to now, she'd always thought of as being an experience that lay ahead of her. Something to look foward to, in the future. Not when she'd just achieved the first, great success of her career. And most definitely *not* when her brief love affair with the baby's father had proved so disastrously short.

But whatever happened, she definitely was going to keep her baby. Now for the One Million Dollar Question: what was she going to do about Matt?

EXPECTING

She's sexy,
successful...
and
PREGNANT!

Relax and enjoy our new series of stories about
spirited women and gorgeous men, whose
passion results in pregnancies...sometimes
unexpected! Of course, the birth of a baby is
always a joyful event, and we can guarantee that
our characters will become besotted moms and
dads—but what happened in those nine
months before?

Share the surprises, emotions, dramas and
suspense as our parents-to-be come to terms
with the prospect of bringing a new little life into
the world.... All will discover that the business of
making babies brings with it the most special
love of all....

Look out next month for:
Accidental Baby by Kim Lawrence
Harlequin Presents® #2034

MARY LYONS

The Playboy's Baby

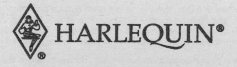

HARLEQUIN®

TORONTO • NEW YORK • LONDON
AMSTERDAM • PARIS • SYDNEY • HAMBURG
STOCKHOLM • ATHENS • TOKYO • MILAN • MADRID
PRAGUE • WARSAW • BUDAPEST • AUCKLAND

ISBN 0-373-12028-1

THE PLAYBOY'S BABY

First North American Publication 1999.

CHAPTER ONE

'WELL, young lady, we're certainly all looking forward to hearing your presentation this afternoon.'

The grey-haired chairman of one of the largest corporate businesses in America smiled down at the slim blonde girl standing beside him. 'I understand that you are intending to tell us all about the European Bond Market,' he added with a distinct twinkle in his eye.

'Well…er…' Samantha Thomas cleared her throat nervously, desperately trying to think of what to say to this well-known and highly distinguished man, who quite obviously knew far more about the subject than she did.

What on earth was she doing here, in New York? she asked herself, feeling sick with nerves as she tried to control the small coffee cup and saucer from rattling in her trembling hands.

How could she have been such an idiot as to even *think* of agreeing to give a keynote speech at this financial seminar? Especially when she ought to have known that it would be attended by so many high-powered bankers and economists—*all* of whom were obviously far more intelligent and successful than she could ever hope to be.

However, as if able to read her mind, the elderly businessman gave her a friendly pat on the shoulder.

'When you've been in the job as long as I have,' he said, 'you'll realise that no one is so smart—or so clever—that he or she can't learn something new, every day. So, don't worry. I'm sure that you'll do just fine,' he added with an encouraging smile, before his attention was claimed by a group of corporate tax lawyers on the other side of the small ante-room.

Allowing a passing waiter to pour her another cup of strong coffee, Samantha made a determined effort to pull herself together. After all, she would never have been asked to speak at this prestigious conference if the organisers had felt she was likely to make a fool of herself. And besides, she *was* now in charge of her own team, in the UK pension fund department at Minerva Utilities Management, in London. Right? All the same...

Her gloomy, nervous thoughts were interrupted as she heard her name being called out by Candy, one of the assistants to the conference organiser, as she quickly wove her way towards Samantha through the crowd of people.

'I'm so sorry that I had to rush off halfway through lunch!' Candy exclaimed hurriedly. 'Unfortunately, there's been a bit of a problem with this afternoon's seminar. The person who *was* supposed to be introducing your talk was taken ill late last night. So, my boss has been on the phone all morning, trying to find a replacement. However...it's been sorted out now. And it's all thanks to *you*,' Candy added with a laugh. 'You certainly seem to have some friends in high places!'

Feeling slightly bewildered by the rapid, breathless flow of words, Samantha struggled to make sense of what the other girl had been saying.

'I don't understand... What "friends in high places"? I hardly know anyone in New York.'

'Oh, yeah? That's not what I hear!' Candy grinned. 'So, what is it with you and the glamorous Mr Matthew Warner?'

'Mr Matthew Warner?' Sam echoed blankly, her brain in a complete daze for a moment as she stared open-mouthed at the dark-haired girl standing beside her. 'Well...yes, I did once know someone of that name. But...but that was in England. And a very, very long time ago. I'm sorry, but I think...well, I really think you must be mistaken.'

'Oh, really?' Candy grinned again. 'Well, it seems that Mr Warner certainly remembers *you*. In fact, he was categorically refusing to help us out until my boss faxed over your CV to his office. And then, what do you know? *Hey Presto!* His personal assistant phones to say that he'd be delighted to chair the meeting—*and* to renew his acquaintance with an old friend.'

Samantha's head was still spinning as the other girl gave her a quick dig in the ribs.

'Uh-huh! Look—there he is. Standing by the door, on the other side of the room,' Candy muttered out of the side of her mouth. 'And if you *have* managed to forget such a gorgeous man—I reckon you must need your head examined!' she added with a muffled laugh. 'Not only tall, dark, handsome and incredibly rich—but also, I hear on the grapevine, currently unattached. What *more* could any girl ask for in her Christmas stocking?'

'It's still only April—so you've got a long time to wait,' Sam found herself muttering inanely as she turned to look across the room.

'Who cares?' Candy giggled. 'I'd be happy to have *him* delivered gift-wrapped any time of the year!'

But Samantha wasn't listening. Every ounce of her being was concentrated on focusing on the tall, dark man standing in the doorway, clearly relaxed and at ease as his gaze travelled slowly around the chattering groups of people in the small room. And then, as their eyes met, he stood very still for a moment before giving a slight nod of wry acknowledgement as he began walking slowly through the crowd towards her.

Her first, overriding thought was that someone had obviously made a bad mistake. It couldn't *possibly* be the man to whom she'd lost her heart all those years ago.

For one thing, Warner was a fairly common surname. And besides, the Matthew Warner whom she'd known had been a young lecturer at Oxford University—normally clothed in scruffy jeans and a well-worn, slightly

threadbare jacket, like most of his academic contempo-
raries. Absolutely *light years* away from this immacu-
lately dressed, distinguished-looking man who was now
strolling so coolly and confidently towards her.

And yet...well, maybe there *was* something disturbingly familiar about the tall, elegant stranger...?

As he drew nearer, Samantha was almost physically
aware of the colour draining from her face. Her senses,
clearly far more alert than her dazed mind, instinctively
responding as she felt her stomach give a sudden, sick-
ening lurch of fear and recognition, her pulse beginning
to race out of control as he came to a halt in front of her
nervous, trembling figure.

'Hello, Sam. It's been a long time, hasn't it?'

Samantha was rigid with shock, and it was some moments before she was able to comprehend the evidence
of her own eyes and ears. And then she knew, with absolute certainty, that there was no possibility of a mistake.

While she might have been momentarily fooled by the
expensive, hand-tailored dark suit, pristine white silk shirt
and discreet silk tie, there was no disguising that oh, so
familiar, deep, husky tone of voice.

Oh, my God! It really *was* Matt Warner, his green eyes
beneath their heavy lids glinting with wry amusement as
he gazed down at her stunned expression—the very last
man in the world she had ever expected, or wanted, to
see.

Well...certainly not here, in New York. And most definitely not *now*—just as she was about to give the most
important speech of her life.

It simply wasn't fair! Samantha told herself bitterly,
standing silently by as Candy quickly grabbed the opportunity to introduce herself. If she'd ever hoped to meet
up again with the man who'd so cruelly broken her
heart—and, being only human, of course she had—she
could never have devised such a disastrous scenario.

Her favourite fantasy had tended to revolve around the

idea of Matt—by now reduced to begging a living outside the Royal Opera House in Covent Garden—humbly grateful for the coin idly thrown his way as she, dressed up to the nines, swept past him on the arm of a handsome, mega-rich captain of industry. It had most definitely *not* involved her standing here, wearing a boringly conventional, navy blue business suit, and totally paralysed with nerves. For heaven's sake—was there *no* justice in this world?

'And how long are you staying in town?'

Rapidly struggling to pull herself together, Samantha realised that she'd hardly heard a word he'd been saying.

'I...er...I'm just here for a few d-days,' she stuttered helplessly, her mind still in a chaotic daze.

His lips twitching with amusement at her evident confusion, Matt asked where she was staying—nodding approval at her choice of the Mark Hotel, on East Seventy-seventh Street.

'They'll certainly make sure that you are well looked after. So, what do you think of New York?'

'It's an amazing place...so alive and exciting,' she murmured distractedly, before giving a helpless shrug of her slim shoulders. 'I'm sorry, Matt. I don't seem to be able to concentrate on anything just at the moment. I mean...it's really great to see you after all these years. But unfortunately I'm just about to give a speech. In front of all these really important people. And...and I've never felt quite so nervous in all my life!' she gabbled wildly, the coffee cup and saucer clattering like a pair of castanets in her nervous, shaking hands.

In what seemed the twinkling of an eye, Matthew Warner quickly took control of the situation. Smoothly dismissing Candy with a charming smile, he calmly steered Samantha towards a small bar at the end of the room, where he proceeded to order her a glass of neat brandy.

'Are you crazy?' she exclaimed in horror. 'The next

thing you know, I'll be had up for being drunk in charge of a podium!'

'Rubbish! Drink it up,'' he retorted.

'It's all very well for you,' she protested, ashamed to find herself weakly doing as she was told. '*You* haven't got to stand up in a few moments' time and make an absolute fool of yourself before some of the cleverest financial minds in New York. I just know that it's going to be an absolute *disaster*!' she added helplessly, feeling almost faint with nervous tension.

'Nonsense!' he told her firmly. 'Not only were you my best and brightest pupil all those years ago. But, if your current CV is anything to go by, it looks as though you've been moving swiftly up the corporate ladder, and achieving considerable success in your field.'

'Well, yes, I suppose so.' Samantha gave an embarrassed shrug of her shoulders, ashamed to have been caught off-guard and exposing herself to ridicule—by Matt, of all people.

Unfortunately, it wasn't just the fact that her stomach seemed to be churning around like a cement mixer out of control, which was making her feel so peculiar. The close proximity of this man, whom she hadn't seen for such a long time, didn't seem to be doing a damn thing for her normally calm, stable equilibrium, either. Maybe another quick glance at her speech—which she'd spent hours writing last night—would help to steady her nerves?

'I don't want to hear any more of this ''poor little me'' nonsense,' Matt was saying, a warm smile taking the sting out of his words as she extracted the typewritten pages from her handbag. 'And, believe me, that's definitely a bad mistake.'

'What?' She glanced up at him in confusion.

'Are those the notes for the speech you're intending to give this afternoon?'

'Yes. I just thought that... *Hey!* What the hell do you

think you're doing?' she exclaimed as he swiftly removed the papers from her hands.

'I take it that you *do* know what you're going to be talking about?' he drawled, leafing quickly through the closely typed pages.

'Of course I do!' she snapped angrily, the strong, heady fumes of the brandy beginning to flow swiftly through her veins.

'Well, in that case, you'll have no need of these,' he said, ignoring her gasp of horror as he swiftly tore the white pages in half. 'With everything you have to say clearly in your mind,' Matt added firmly, 'there's absolutely no point in allowing yourself to be distracted by continually being forced to consult your notes.'

'Oh, great! Thanks—for absolutely *nothing*!' she hissed furiously. 'So, what the hell am I supposed to do now?'

'What you're going to do, my dear Sam, is to walk in there and give the speech of your life,' he drawled, taking hold of her arm and leading her slowly across the room as they followed the other guests towards the conference hall.

'I'll never forgive you for this,' she ground out savagely. 'Absolutely never!'

He gave a low, maddening chuckle of sardonic laughter. 'Oh, yes, you will! In fact, I fully expect to receive your grateful thanks, when I take you out to dinner tonight.'

'In your dreams!' she snorted with derision.

'Well, yes...' he murmured, turning to look at the slim figure of the girl walking beside him, his glance travelling over the shining mass of pale gold hair caught up in a knot at the crown of her head, a few tendrils escaping to frame her lightly tanned, heart-shaped face and large blue eyes. 'Yes, I think you could be right,' he added enigmatically.

'However, in the meantime,' he continued firmly, 'all

you have to do is to take a deep breath—and then sock
it to 'em. Believe me, you're going to be a great success.'

Entering her hotel bedroom, Samantha tossed her handbag
on to a nearby chair, before quickly slipping off her shoes
and throwing herself down on the thick mattress of the
comfortable, king-sized bed.

Phew! What a day this had turned out to be, she told
herself, closing her eyes and allowing the strain and tension of the past few hours to seep gradually from her
exhausted mind and body.

However galling it might be, she had to admit that Matt
had been quite right, after all. Without the safety-net of
written notes, she'd had no choice but to stand on the dais
in front of so many people and, as he'd so graphically
put it, 'sock it to 'em'.

At the start of the afternoon session, as she'd sat beside
him on the dais, desperately trying to ignore her sheer
terror and stage fright, it had been some moments before
Samantha had begun to realise that she was indeed very
lucky to have Matt chairing the meeting.

From the moment he'd risen to his feet, welcoming the
delegates and making one or two glancing references to
events on Wall Street—which had left her completely baf-
fled, but produced gales of laughter from the audience—
he'd had everyone relaxed, cheerful and eating out of his
hand.

So much so, that, when it was time to take her place
on the podium, Samantha had finally managed to get a
grip on herself. Suddenly realising that she *did* know what
she was talking about, and with everyone apparently ea-
ger to hear what she had to say, she'd found no problem
in getting her message across to the assembled company.

At the close of her speech, her ears had been ringing
with applause as she left the dais. Trembling with a mixture of exhaustion and exhilaration, she'd found herself
totally surrounded by a crowd of people. In fact she had

been so busy—both accepting congratulations and answering the many questions raised by her speech—that she'd somehow lost sight of Matt. And unfortunately, by the time she'd managed to catch her breath and look about her, he'd been nowhere to be seen.

Feeling extremely guilty, since she really *did* owe him an enormous vote of thanks, there had been nothing she could do about the situation, other than allow herself to be chauffeured back to her hotel.

But now, as she sat bolt upright on the bed, she was dismayed to realise that she had no way of contacting Matt. She didn't know where he lived. She hadn't a clue as to the name of his business—or the location of his office. Nor, come to that, had she any idea of what he was doing here, in the United States.

Bitterly ashamed of having been so preoccupied with her own problems this afternoon that she'd completely failed to show any interest in Matt's affairs—or to enquire what had happened to him during the past eight or nine years—she wondered what on earth she could do to rectify the situation.

After spending some moments buried in thought, Samantha soon realised that the only person who could help her was Candy.

Unfortunately, a quick glance at her bedside clock told her that it was now six-thirty on a Friday night. The other girl would obviously have left her office by now. Which meant that Samantha had no way of contacting her, or the organisation which had arranged the seminar, until first thing on Monday morning. And since she, herself, was due to fly back to England on Monday evening, she would have virtually no opportunity either to see Matt again or to thank him for his kindness and support this afternoon.

Still…maybe it was just as well. After all, despite what that silly girl Candy had said about Matt being 'unattached', it was virtually certain that such a handsome, attractive man would be either married—or heavily involved in a current, romantic relationship.

Besides...despite her total preoccupation with her own problems, the way her nerve-ends had been tingling during their brief encounter this afternoon wasn't exactly good news. So, it was probably best—for her own peace of mind, anyway—that they should have no more contact with one another.

Despite having given herself such very good advice, Samantha lay back on the pillows desperately trying to control a sudden cloud of dark depression. Of course, there *had* been other men in her life—not to mention that brief, disastrous marriage which she'd made on the rebound from her romance with Matt. However, she'd never again experienced such an intense, profound depth of emotion as she'd once felt for the man who had so unexpectedly reappeared in her life.

Pull yourself together! she told herself roughly. That had all been a very long time ago—when she'd been as green as grass, and deeply in the throes of her first love affair. Her life was very different, nowadays.

And she had so much to be thankful for: a job which she loved and a glamorous, penthouse loft apartment which—despite having cost an arm and a leg—was proving to be a splendid capital investment. She was also the proud possessor of a speedy little BMW, and was earning what her parents and two sisters regarded as a totally *indecent* amount of money.

So, who needed love, romance and all that heavy stuff? Especially since it would only detract from her single-minded and whole-hearted devotion to her career. Oh, yes—she was now fully in control of her own destiny.

Just as she was assuring herself that she had a totally satisfactory lifestyle—and that an attractive and sexy man was the very *last* thing she needed in her life, at the moment—the fax machine on the desk across the room suddenly began to clatter.

This really was a wonderful hotel, Samantha told herself as she slowly rolled off the bed. Whilst cushioning its guests in total luxury, the Mark also had the added bonus of providing what was virtually an individual office in each bedroom. As well as the fax and phone on the Chippendale-style desk, there were also plugs and ports for her laptop computer, and any other fancy gismo which she might care to use.

All of which meant that she was able to keep in constant contact with her office, back in London, through phone, fax and e-mail. Although she was surprised that her office should be contacting her, since it must be about midnight in London. What sort of crisis could have blown up at this late hour? she wondered, frowning as she removed the message from the fax machine.

But it wasn't from her office in London. Samantha's eyes widened as she noted the name at the top of the page. Even she, unfamiliar as she was with the financial rating of American big business, knew that Broadwood Securities Inc. was one of the largest companies in the United States. Her eyes widened even further as she noted that the letter bore the signature of one Matthew Warner: chairman and chief executive.

She gave an incredulous whistle. *Oh, wow!* It looked as if Candy had been quite right, after all. Because it was now clear that Matt was definitely a big cheese on Wall Street. No *wonder* everyone in the audience, this afternoon, had been hanging on his every word!

In fact, it was rather depressing to realise that maybe her speech hadn't really been *quite* so great, after all. Since she'd been heavily endorsed by one of the prime movers and shakers of the business world, it would have been a miracle if she *hadn't* been listened to with serious attention.

Well, that's put you in your place, my girl! Samantha told herself ruefully, before belatedly reading the rest of the letter, which was brief and to the point. Reminding her of his invitation, earlier this afternoon, Matt had made arrangements to take her out to dinner at the Four Seasons, and would be picking her up from the hotel at seven-thirty this evening.

Arrogant swine! For all *he* knew, she could be knee-deep in invitations for this evening. And, for at least five seconds, Samantha seriously considered faxing back a message, telling him to get lost!

However, swiftly recalling her need to thank Matt for his efforts this afternoon—quite apart from the fact that she really *did* want to see him again—Samantha glanced down at her watch, before giving a quick yelp of dismay. She only had about three-quarters of an hour in which to not only wash and dry her long hair, but also to find something ultra-smart to wear. Because even she, who hardly knew New York, was well aware that the Four Seasons was one of the most glamorous restaurants in the city.

Just over half an hour later, Samantha was regarding herself anxiously in the huge mirror in the bathroom.

Having only packed a few suitable clothes for what was, as far as she'd been aware, nothing more than a business trip, she could only thank her lucky stars that she had, at the last minute, tossed into her suitcase this little black dress. But was it too plain and boring?

A very simple sheath of black silk crêpe, which had been a mainstay of her wardrobe for the past few years, it was hardly likely to set the world on fire! Even the single row of pearls, while emphasising her long, slim neck, couldn't manage to make an inexpensive dress look a million dollars.

Still…what the heck? There was absolutely no point in worrying too much about her ensemble, since there was virtually nothing she could do about it. And if Matt thought she didn't look smart enough—well, that was just too bad.

However, from Matt's appreciative glance, as he ran

his eyes over her slim figure and long, freshly washed blonde hair, falling in a pale stream of liquid gold down over her shoulders, he didn't seem *too* disappointed as, at precisely seven-thirty, he ushered her through the front door of the hotel, and into his chauffeur-driven limousine.

With its comfortable chairs and tables arranged around a glamorous marble pool, the restaurant was certainly living up to its reputation for being one of the 'in' places to eat in New York.

But what no one had ever told her, Samantha thought, gazing around at the soft lighting, the shimmering silver beads over the windows and the discreet waiters gliding silently around the room, was just how very romantic it all was. But maybe that was because, for her, the whole evening was fast taking on an air of unreality and increasing enchantment.

How could she have guessed that, despite the passage of so many years, both she and Matt would still seem to be on exactly the same wavelength, as if absolutely *nothing* had changed between them?

But, of course, that couldn't possibly be true. Not when they'd gone their different ways, for such a long time. Which meant that she was going to have to be very careful.

The fact that they were both laughing at the same silly jokes, and actively enjoying snippets of business gossip about low doings in high places, didn't really mean that much in the scheme of things. And if she was totally astounded to find that she *still* found him devastatingly attractive and—to be utterly frank—had difficulty suppressing an insane desire to throw herself into his arms, it was highly unlikely that he felt the same way.

Unfortunately, she hadn't a clue as to exactly *what* Matt was thinking. Cool, calm and utterly charming, he was clearly setting out to give her an enjoyable evening. But, even while relating how, as a young professor at

Oxford, he'd been head-hunted by an American bank, intent on setting up an economic 'think tank' to look at future economic trends—before recently joining his present company as chairman and chief executive—he gave no sign of how he felt about her, or their past relationship.

It was no wonder that their passionate affair had ended in tears, Samantha acknowledged with a heavy, inward sigh. Any romantic attachment between young students and their older professors had always been heavily frowned on by the university authorities. And now, with the aid of hindsight, she could see that Matt had undoubtedly acted quite correctly, both to protect his own academic position and also her future career.

However, the fact that she'd been utterly devastated when he'd so abruptly and cruelly terminated their relationship didn't seem to make any difference. He was still, for her, the most attractive man she'd ever known.

Oh, Lord! Maybe it was the amount of wine which she'd consumed which was causing her to feel so incredibly weak and light-headed? Whatever the reason, she must...she really *must* pull herself together, Samantha told herself desperately, her fingers tightening convulsively around the stem of her delicate, crystal wine goblet as she struggled to clear her mind.

Unfortunately, it was proving extremely difficult to do so. How could she hope to banish the increasingly erotic, sensual memories, when they were sitting so close to one another? She was only human, for heaven's sake! Every slight movement of Matt's tall figure—each accidental brush of his hand, or the lightest touch of his powerful thigh against her own—made it virtually impossible not to recall the hot, fiery excitement of their lovemaking, all those years ago.

'OK, Sam.' His voice broke into her distracted thoughts. 'That's quite enough about me. What have *you* been doing for the past nine years?' Matt drawled with a quizzical gleam in his eyes.

'Well...' she began, taking a deep breath and frantically attempting to ignore the almost overpowering, rampant sex appeal of this highly disturbing man. 'It's been madly hectic, of course. I'm now managing the pension funds of several large companies, and—'

'No, that's not what I meant.' He interrupted her with a quick, dismissive wave of his long, tanned fingers. 'I'm far more interested in your *private* life. For instance, I noted that there was no mention of a husband on your CV...?'

'Well...' she murmured, before taking a long, slow sip of her wine, her brain racing swiftly into overdrive as she frantically tried to think of an answer to his question.

How on earth, at this stage of the evening, could she possibly tell Matt the truth? He was bound to want to know what lay behind the break-up of her very brief, utterly disastrous marriage.

Agreeing to wed the painter, Alan Gifford, while still madly in love with Matt, had to be absolutely the *worst* decision she'd ever taken. On the rebound from their passionate affair, and still suffering from the agony and torment of his brutal rejection, she clearly hadn't been in her right mind. How else to explain the fact that she had *known* her marriage was doomed, even as she'd walked down the aisle? That her predominant impulse had been an infantile desire to show Matt that she didn't care. That even if *he* didn't want her, or still find her attractive, there were plenty of men out there who did.

Oh, no...it was all *far* too embarrassing. She simply *couldn't* face the shame of telling Matt what a fool she'd been. And definitely not here and now...in this glamorous restaurant. Surely the last place in which to relate such a miserably unhappy period in her life.

Despite knowing that she might well come to bitterly regret not telling him the truth—and deliberately closing her mind to the small voice of sanity, predicting trouble in store—Samantha took a deep breath and shook her head.

'No…I'm not married,' she said, comforting herself with the thought that she was, in fact, speaking the absolute truth. 'I've obviously had some serious boyfriends, of course, but…'

'Well, yes…I should think so,' he drawled smoothly, his deeply hooded green eyes sweeping over her lovely face and long, newly washed blonde hair. 'Is there anyone important in your life at the moment?'

'No…er…not really,' she muttered, bitterly aware of her cheeks reddening as she tried to avoid his gaze. Swiftly deciding to turn the spotlight away from herself, she asked, 'And what about you?'

'I'm still single,' he told her. 'Although I've obviously had quite a few girlfriends over the past few years…'

I just bet you have! Samantha thought grimly, ashamed to discover that she wasn't immune from the acid green, needle-sharp pangs of sour jealousy. Which was absolutely crazy, considering both her own marriage and the fact that it was so long since she and Matt had seen one another.

'And I have had a long-standing relationship with someone for the past three years.'

'Oh, really?' she murmured, doing her best to respond to his words with a warm, friendly smile. Quite determined—even if it killed her!—to appear happy to hear that he had a live-in lover, Samantha added brightly, 'Maybe she ought to have joined us here for dinner tonight? In any case, you really *must* introduce me to your girlfriend when I'm next in New York.'

'No, well, I'm afraid that might prove to be just a bit difficult,' Matt drawled, his green eyes gleaming with amusement. 'Because that particular relationship has recently been terminated.'

'Oh, dear. I'm very sorry to hear that,' she told him, privately appalled at how shockingly easy it was to suddenly become a barefaced liar. 'What...er...what led to the break-up?'

Matt shrugged his broad shoulders. 'It was entirely my fault, I'm afraid. Because when it came to the point of having to make some sort of permanent commitment, such as marriage, I suddenly realised that I couldn't quite go the distance.'

He paused for a moment, before adding reflectively, 'I suppose the harsh truth is that I discovered, in the nick of time, that I didn't wish to spend the rest of my life with that particular lady.' He gave another slight shrug. 'So that was it. End of story.'

'I'm sorry that it didn't work out for you.'

'There's no need to be sorry,' he grinned. 'Quite frankly—just between the two of us—I rather think that I've had a lucky escape!

'In any case, that's all in the past,' Matt continued firmly. 'In fact, my dear Sam, I'd say that it's both the present and the immediate future which looks far more promising. What do you think?'

You've got to get a grip on the situation! Samantha yelled silently at her weak, inner self as he attracted the attention of a waiter, and began settling the bill for their meal.

For heaven's sake—she was certainly old enough to know when a guy was coming on to her. But, having spent the past two hours desperately trying to ignore this man's overwhelming, dark attraction, she was now in such a state of tense, nervous exhaustion that she simply wasn't capable of adding two and two—let alone able to guess what he had in mind for the rest of the evening.

'I...er...I'm not quite sure what you mean,' she muttered, when the waiter had left and they were alone once more.

'Oh, come on, Sam!' He raised one dark eyebrow, his eyes gleaming with amusement as he gave her a wry,

mocking smile. 'I mean that I think it's definitely time
we adjourned to my apartment, don't you?'

Ah! Even her bemused mind was beginning to get the
message by now—loud and clear! But he was going to
have to spell it out. And in words of one syllable, she
told herself tersely. After all, it was *he* who'd dumped
her, all those years ago. So, there was no way she was
going to make the first move. *Absolutely not!*

'And what exactly do you have in mind, Matt?' she
queried, as lightly as possible, although she'd never felt
so on edge, or so jittery, in all her life.

He gave a low rumble of deeply sensual laughter.
'Now, that's what I've always loved about you, Sam!' he
drawled, firmly clasping her nervous, trembling fingers.

'It's good to know you haven't changed. That you're
still not interested in messing around, or playing games—
but believe in keeping your eye firmly on the main issue
for discussion! Right?' he added as he raised her trembling hand to his warm lips.

'Oh, Matt...' she muttered helplessly, a deep flush
spreading over her pale cheeks.

'Relax, darling!' he murmured, still keeping a firm grip
on her fingers, his green eyes glinting with sardonic
amusement. 'I can, of course, offer you a drink or a cup
of coffee. However, I'd much rather indulge in a bout of
mad, passionate lovemaking. A fact, I may say, which
has been at the very top of my agenda since approximately two o'clock this afternoon! How's that for plain
speaking?'

'Not bad!' She grinned, suddenly feeling quite amazingly happy. And then, as he stared down at her, the
gleam in his eyes carrying an unmistakable message, the
slowly churning excitement in her stomach seemed to
burst into a hot surge of overwhelming sexual desire,
causing her to feel almost faint as it raged fiercely through
her quivering body.

'So, like all good financial experts, I'd say that it's

definitely about time we began to discuss the present company's imminent merger,' Matt said as he rose to his feet. 'Not to mention the pressing need to *very* closely examine the figures concerned!' he added in a slow drawl, the thick, husky note in his voice positively making her toes curl as he turned to help her rise from the table. 'What do you think, hmm...?'

It was some moments before Samantha—by now practically speechless with overriding lust and passion—somehow managed to get her act together.

'I don't seem to have a problem with that *particular* item on the...er...the agenda of tonight's meeting,' she murmured breathlessly as Matt took her arm and led her slowly out of the restaurant.

CHAPTER TWO

SAMANTHA'S heart was pounding like a sledgehammer, her pulse rate rocketing all over the place as she left the Four Seasons restaurant on Matt's arm.

In what seemed a dream-like state, totally oblivious of everyone and everything, other than the tall, handsome figure by her side, she was only vaguely conscious of being helped into a large black limousine. As they were swiftly transported through brilliantly lit streets, she had no idea of where they were going. Nor did she care. Just as long as Matt continued to hold her firmly close to his hard, exciting body—they could have been jetting off to Timbuktu, for all she knew!

Coming to a halt at last outside an immensely large, brownstone building, she had only a brief impression of a uniformed doorman greeting Matt before he swept her dazed figure across a vast entrance hall—the only sound in the huge, silent space being the rapid, sharp click of her high-heeled evening sandals on the marble floor—and into an elevator. And then, in what seemed the twinkling of an eye, Matt was unlocking the front door of his apartment.

'Welcome to my humble abode,' he drawled sardonically as he helped her off with her coat, before ushering her into a huge living room.

Finding herself standing in the midst of what seemed positively *acres* of lush, thickly piled cream carpeting, Samantha could only stare in open-mouthed astonishment at her luxurious surroundings. The opulent, heavy gilt rococo 'French Château comes to New York via

Hollywood' style of decoration could only be described as utterly mind-blowing!

'Make yourself comfortable by the fire,' Matt directed, picking up a small black handset and pointing it at various objects as he strode towards a mahogany bar on the far side of the room.

Coming slowly back down to earth, she was just wondering how on earth he could bear to live in such dreadful surroundings, when she was startled to see the heavy cream silk, intricately draped curtains being slowly drawn—as if by invisible hands—across the windows, to shut out the chilly darkness of the April night. At the same time, the lamps in the crystal chandeliers slowly dimmed, the brilliant light being replaced by a soft, warm glow from the many occasional lamps dotted about the huge room.

However, when the logs in the massive grate, enclosed by an intricately carved marble mantelpiece, suddenly burst into life she quickly realised that what had at first appeared to be minor miracles were, in fact, merely a result of the appliance of science.

'Is everything in this "humble abode" operated by remote control?' she queried, her legs feeling wobbly with nerves as she moved slowly over to the fireplace.

'No, not entirely. There are still one or two things which I'm *quite* capable of doing myself!' Matt told her with a grin, his words accompanied by a loud crack as he removed the cork from a bottle of champagne.

'It's definitely all very…er…very grand,' she murmured, gazing bemusedly at the delicately ornate, highly uncomfortable-looking sofas and chairs covered in blue silk which filled the room—whose walls, covered in dark oil paintings, appeared to be lined in the same blue material.

'Ghastly, isn't it?' he laughed, filling two tall glasses with sparkling gold liquid.

'Well…'

'Following my recent appointment as chief executive of the company, I was working practically twenty-four hours a day when I first bought this apartment—which was in a terrible state and badly needed doing up. So, I made the grave error of placing its renovation in the hands of my ex-girlfriend—supposedly a top-notch professional decorator. The rest of the apartment is fine. So why she went so completely over the top in *this* room is completely beyond me.

'Unfortunately,' he added quickly as a mobile phone on the bar beside him gave an imperious buzz, 'I simply haven't been able to find the time to clear everything out and start again.'

While he was speaking rapidly into the phone, dealing with some urgent business matter which clearly required an immediate decision, Samantha became aware that the fog in her brain was slowly beginning to dissolve.

Sobering up fast, she realised that in accompanying Matt back here, to this luridly decorated apartment of his, she could have made a really bad, foolish mistake.

For one thing, it was *never* a good idea to try and recapture the past. Everyone knew that. So, why on earth had she allowed herself to be swept along on this tide of sudden, overwhelming lust and desire—which could so easily turn into nothing more than a highly embarrassing encounter?

Besides…this room was *so* awful, it seemed highly unlikely that a 'top-notch' interior designer would ever produce such a ghastly decorative scheme. Not unless the lady concerned had deliberately planned a not so subtle, bitter revenge against her ex-boyfriend.

Matt, as well as being a successful businessman, was clearly a bit of a playboy. He'd also admitted, in the restaurant, that he was definitely not into 'commitment'. Which meant that it would be extremely unwise, Samantha told herself nervously, to get involved with someone who'd managed to provoke such a very ruthless, savage reaction from his discarded girlfriend.

So much water had flowed under the bridge since she'd first fallen head over heels in love with this man. Which *had* to mean that they were now two quite different people. Therefore, any idea that somehow time might have stood still—or that they could simply take up their relationship at the point where it had been broken off—was nothing more than total moonshine!

'I'm sorry about that,' Matt said as he finished his call, and tossed his mobile phone down on to a nearby chair. 'I've turned the damned thing off—so we shouldn't have any more interruptions,' he added, walking across the room towards her.

'This room has very good proportions,' she observed nervously as he handed her a tall glass of champagne. 'I mean...there must be many other good...er...good interior designers in New York. So, it shouldn't be too hard to turn it into a...um...a comfortable home.'

Appalled to hear herself gabbling like an idiot, she took a quick sip of the deliciously cold, fizzy golden liquid—desperately trying to ignore the way her body was now responding with nervous, tingling excitement to the close proximity of his tall, lean figure.

If it were anyone else, she wouldn't have a problem. It was just Matt and their past history together...which must be the reason why she was suddenly feeling as jumpy as hell. So, the smart move must be to try to extricate herself from this tricky situation—as swiftly as possible.

'Good heavens—just look at the time!' she exclaimed shrilly, pointedly turning to glance at an ornate French clock, on a spindly side table. 'I hadn't realised it was quite so late. I...er...I really think that I should...'

'*I* really think that you should calm down,' he drawled smoothly, placing his glass down on the mantelpiece.

'Nonsense! I'm perfectly calm,' she snapped, utterly

exhausted by the frantic pounding of her heart and yet, at the same time, feeling so desperately tense and on edge that it seemed as though she'd never again be able to relax.

But his only reply was a toe-curling, low rumble of laughter as he slipped an arm about her slender waist, deftly removing the tall champagne flute from her shaky fingers and placing it beside his own glass, before putting his other arm about her trembling body.

'Relax, sweetheart!' he murmured huskily, raising a hand to brush a stray lock of hair from her brow softly.

Shivering at the velvety touch of his fingers on her skin, which were now trailing slowly down over the long line of her neck, a rush of heat seemed to scorch through her veins, her stomach muscles clenching into a hard knot of feverish desire as he began pulling her closer to his tall figure.

Gazing helplessly up at him, she could see a muscle beating in his jaw, a slight flush on the high cheekbones beneath his tanned skin, with the glittering green eyes beneath their heavy lids now growing cloudy and opaque as he stared down at the trembling lips and the confused, troubled expression on her face.

'I'm sorry, Matt. I...I know you must think that I'm an utter fool,' she confessed in a husky, breathless voice. 'But...'

'On the contrary,' he murmured thickly. 'I think you're sensationally attractive, and a very, *very* sexy lady.'

'But, I shouldn't have come back here, to your apartment. It's impossible to try and recapture the past,' she protested. 'Quite honestly, we...we could both be making a bad mistake.'

'I've certainly made some wrong decisions in my life—but this definitely *isn't* one of them,' he told her flatly, the hard certainty in his voice sending shivers down her backbone.

'No, you're not thinking it through!' she gasped.

He gave a low snort of derisory laughter. 'I'm not interested in "thinking" about anything, at the moment. I just need to hold you…to feel you…'

'Matt! This *really* isn't a good idea,' she muttered helplessly, aware that her body was denying her words of caution; that her swelling breasts and the visible hardening of her nipples were clearly signalling the rising tide of sensual need and passion, now sweeping through her trembling figure. But, quite unable to do anything about it, she could only gaze weakly up at the tanned face, now only inches away from her own.

'Believe me, this is just about the *only* idea I've had since first setting eyes on you this afternoon.'

His deep, husky voice seemed to echo around the large room, time standing still as his arms slowly tightened about her.

And then, with sudden impatience, he pulled her hard up against his firmly muscled body, before lowering his dark head and possessing her lips in a long-drawn-out kiss of overwhelming sensuality.

At the first touch of his warm lips on hers, there could be no denying that this was what she had been both hungering for and yet, at the same time, fearing since first setting eyes on him this afternoon. She was powerless, totally unable to do anything other than eagerly respond to the mouth moving over her lips with insidious persuasion, gently forcing and probing them apart with a deeply erotic, seductive arousal that totally inflamed her senses.

Desperately attempting to cling on to some kind of sanity, Samantha felt as though she was helplessly caught up in the forceful tide which was pounding and rampaging through her body; betrayed by a deep compulsion to respond to her overwhelming need of him.

However, as his kiss deepened, it seemed as if some outside agency had suddenly pulled a switch—abruptly releasing a massive torrent of dangerous electricity, violently zigzagging like fork lightning through her body.

And, incredibly, it seemed as if the same explosive force of unstable, super-charged voltage was also sweeping like a flash-flood through his tall frame.

Totally gripped by an ancient, primitive force that was quite beyond either of them to control, all normal and civilised behaviour simply vanished into thin air. With their lips still firmly clasped together, he tore the clothes first from her body, and then his—all their garments being feverishly hurled aside as they wildly sought to satisfy their mutual, overwhelming need.

It was only when she became dimly aware of her naked form being roughly clasped to his bare chest, as he lowered her down on to the thick white rug in front of the fire, that she made a last, despairing attempt to cling on to sanity.

'This is crazy...we must be out of our minds...' she gasped as he covered her soft naked flesh with his own hard, firm body.

'For God's sake!' he breathed thickly, his hands sweeping erotically over her trembling figure. 'Are you *really* asking me to stop making love to you? Because if not, my darling,' he added with a muffled laugh, pressing his warm lips to her swollen breasts, 'can we *please* leave any argument about moral ethics and civilised behaviour until later?'

Unable to prevent a deep, responsive shudder from scorching through her body, she found her arms closing instinctively about him, her fingers curling into his thick dark hair as he pressed feverish kisses over her soft, warm flesh.

She wanted him. There was nothing...absolutely *nothing* in this world that she wanted more than the possession of this man. Racked by desire, her body burned and shook, her need of him so intense that it was like a deep, physical pain.

'No, I...I don't want you to stop...' she gasped. 'And yet...'

'Oh, shut up, Sam!' he groaned, before effectively putting a stop to any more of her hesitant protests, his mouth crushing her lips in a long, deeply sensual kiss of rampant possession.

A soft moan broke from her throat as she yielded to the intensity of his kiss, the sound provoking a deep, shuddering convulsion in the body pressed so closely to her own. And then she was lost, firmly in the grip of a basic, primeval force that seemed quite beyond both her control and his. There was no time for shame or regret as her fingers savoured the strong contours of his body, the flesh beneath her hands so achingly and poignantly familiar. The savage, raw passion which had been repressed for so long suddenly exploded passionately between them, their bodies merging in a wild, untamed hunger and overpowering need.

Much later, lying warm and drowsily replete, their limbs entwined together on the thick rug in front of the blazing fire, she became aware of Matt's fingers trailing softly up over her body, to turn her face gently towards him.

'Darling...'

'Mmm...?' she muttered sleepily.

Still feeling dazed at the passion which had so completely engulfed them, she was almost unable to believe the frantic intensity of her own reaction to his equally frenzied lovemaking. It seemed as if some wild, dynamic force had taken possession of her mind and body, igniting a fire in her blood which had raged totally out of control.

But now, as the first glimmer of harsh reality began to break through the thick mist in her mind, Samantha became aware of the first definite stirrings of unease.

'Darling Sam,' he said quietly, softly brushing stray locks of damp, pale blonde hair from her brow. 'I hope you're not expecting me to apologise for what's just happened between us. Because I'm damned if I will! It was wonderful, glorious, totally sensational—and virtually inevitable.'

She trembled at the note of certainty in his voice as his arms closed possessively about her body.

Quite suddenly, each and every one of the high barricades and fortifications which she had erected so carefully over the past years now seemed in danger of being entirely swept away. And with them all sense of being in charge of her own destiny. It was frightening to realise that she might now be leaving herself dangerously exposed.

She *had* been deeply in love with Matt, all those years ago. But was it a resurgence of that deep emotion which she was now experiencing—or merely a sudden flash-flood of overwhelming lust? Because there was no point in denying the powerful sexual magnetism which lay between them. But she feared it would prove as unstable and potentially explosive as TNT—merely needing a light spark on the fuse to destructively blow her life apart, yet again.

With the touch of his fingers softly caressing the curves of her warm, naked flesh, it was practically impossible to try to think in a straight line. Even as she struggled to sort out the thoughts crowding into her brain, she found herself being gathered up into Matt's arms and carried down a wide corridor to his bedroom.

'I think we'll both be much more comfortable in here,' he said with a low laugh as he lowered her down on to the wide bed. 'And I don't want any arguments,' he added firmly, rolling her beneath the sheets and joining her a moment later, before once more clasping her in his warm embrace. 'We'll have all the time in the world to talk later, OK?'

But 'talk' did not seem to be anywhere on his agenda when she found herself stirring some hours later, the first pale fingers of dawn gradually seeping in through the light, gauzy curtains at the window, and illuminating the room with a ghostly light.

Drowsily gazing at the unfamiliar surroundings, she turned her head to see Matt slipping silently into bed beside her. And, as he gathered her gently into his arms, she noticed, from the slight dampness of his flesh, that he must have just had a shower.

In a dream-like state, halfway between sleep and waking, she became aware, despite the fresh scent of soap on his skin, of the intoxicating aroma of his own spicy, individual body heat.

Carefully clasping her in his arms as if she was a cherished object, precious beyond compare, he gently kissed her mouth before tenderly trailing his lips down to the scented hollow at the base of her throat. She could feel his breath on her skin, his hands slowly moving down over the warm curves of her body, each lingering caress, each sensual and intimate touch generating tremors of deep pleasure, leaving her aching with the intensity of her need for his possession.

'My darling!' he whispered thickly. 'Right from the first moment I saw you this afternoon—standing so nervously across the room—I suddenly *knew* just what a fool I'd been. It was totally devastating. Like…like being hit by a ten-ton truck!'

'A truck…?' she echoed, so bemused by the thrilling, velvety touch of his fingers on her quivering flesh that she was having difficulty in concentrating on what he was saying.

'I suddenly realised just what a stupid idiot I'd been. We were always so great together. Both mentally and physically. Two halves of one whole. But it couldn't work then, all those years ago…you were so very young…with the whole world in front of you.'

'*Oh, Matt…*'

'I'm absolutely crazy about you, Sam,' he whispered huskily. 'I always was, of course. But now…now we can handle it. We can make it work. In fact, I'll make damn sure it does—because I'm not prepared to let you go again,' he vowed, before giving a low groan of pleasure as he buried his face between the deep valley of her breasts.

As his hoarsely whispered words seemed to hang in the air of the quiet, still room, Samantha could almost physically feel the burden of uncertainty and doubt rolling away, like a great stone from her shoulders, her qualms and hesitant fears dissolving at the deeply sincere note in his voice, and in the direct heat of her own need and desire.

As his hands and mouth moved enticingly over her body, she was filled with wonder and amazement at just how familiar…just how *right* it all seemed, and how equally right Matt had been when he'd said how perfectly their bodies appeared to fit together.

His flesh was sweet and moist and firm as a summer apple. While his groans of delight, and the shudders that rippled through his body in the wake of her own, softly tender touch, as she caressed the oh, so familiar taut muscles and smooth, tanned skin, only served to increase her own pleasure and excitement.

She suddenly realised that making love with Matt again, after so many years, was like returning home from a long voyage, and rediscovering a familiar and intimate joy. And she could only marvel, silently, at why she hadn't always known that it would be so.

In sharp contrast to their earlier, frantic coming together—when they'd been like two people dying of thirst in the desert, who suddenly discovered a lush green oasis—Matt was now slowly savouring her swollen breasts and aching nipples, his fingers and mouth exploring each intimate and private part of her quivering body. As her flesh opened to him like a flower unfolding in the sun, it seemed to her that he moved in love as he did everything else in life, smoothly and easily, clearly tempering the strong, pulsating thrusts of his possession to fit her own rhythm and pleasure, until she became lost to all sense of reality. Her whole existence seemed concentrated on the powerful, exquisite friction; an ever-increasing sense of wild exultation rapidly built up inside her, before the whole world appeared suddenly to explode and disintegrate about them, in shattered fragments of light and power.

When Samantha next opened her eyes, it was to discover bright sunshine flooding through the gauzy bedroom curtains, and Matt's dark head on the pillow beside her.

Careful not to disturb his sleeping form, she eased herself carefully out of bed, before padding silently across the room towards the bathroom. As she had hoped, there was a large white towelling robe hanging on the back of the door. It dwarfed her slim body, of course, but after slipping it on and brushing her teeth with the aid of a brand-new toothbrush, which she'd found in the bathroom cabinet, Samantha decided that she now felt able to face the day.

Locating the kitchen proved to be a more difficult operation. It really was a *huge* apartment. Quite apart from the awful, over-decorated main sitting room, there seemed to be at least two other bedroom suites, and a large study-cum-library.

Luckily, it looked as if his ex-girlfriend, the mad interior designer, had managed to get at least one room right. Standing just inside the door, she gazed around at the walls lined with books, their polished leather bindings in brown, red and green adding a warm glow to the severely masculine lines of a huge mahogany desk, covered in green leather chased in gold, with its matching green leather swivel chair set on a dark grey carpet.

It was clearly a room devoted to quiet, peaceful contemplation, either reading in one of the large, comfortable leather chairs beside the grey marble fireplace, or working at the desk. In fact, it could have been an eighteenth-century gentleman's refuge, were it not for the black telephone, fax and modern laptop computer neatly positioned on the desk.

Feeling slightly ashamed of giving another quick glance around the room—well, Matt *might* have had a photo of his ex-girlfriend still lying around—Samantha firmly pulled herself together, and continued her search for the kitchen.

When she finally tracked it down, she was relieved to note that the large room was a purely functional one.

So, OK, the *very* modern decor—which mainly consisted of glass, and a mass of stainless steel over light oak-coloured floorboards—wasn't everyone's taste. But, since she had no problem with the cool Scandinavian style, she felt perfectly at home. And she was absolutely crazy about the enormous fridge, deeply envious of a piece of equipment which seemed designed to do just about everything except whistle a tune.

In fact, having poured herself some orange juice, she was just experimenting with its ice-making machine, when she nearly jumped out of her skin to hear Matt's voice just behind her.

'Good morning, darling. I was just wondering what had happened to my dressing gown,' he murmured, laughing as she gave a shriek, spilling half the ice cubes on to the floor as she spun around to face him.

'For heaven's sake!' she gasped, quickly bending down to clear up the mess around his bare feet.

'Now…*that's* what I like to see. A woman who knows her place. Which, in this case, appears to be on her knees in the kitchen, before her lord and master. Keep up the good work, Sam!'

'Dream on—O Mighty One!' she retorted with a snort of derisory laughter, gathering up the last ice cubes and rising to her feet.

'Ah, well…bang goes one of my favourite fantasies,'

he drawled with a sardonic grin. 'So, I guess it's back to the real world, hmm?'

'Damn right!' she muttered nervously, evading his eyes as she walked over to the trash can.

She might have pinched his towelling robe, but she did wish he could have found something else to wear, other than that very short towel, wrapped so tightly about his slim hips. Because just at this moment it was desperately important that she keep her wits about her.

While exploring his enormous apartment, she hadn't been able to prevent her mind from see-sawing back and forth, trying to sort out a mass of confused emotions.

Matt had proved to be a warm and generous lover—as well as firmly declaring his deep feelings for her. But she wasn't a starry-eyed young girl any more. And she knew that, while it was easy enough to make promises, and whisper sweet nothings during the height of passion, that same passion had a way of cooling right down to vanishing point in the cold light of day.

More importantly, she wasn't into one-night stands. There had been a time, in the immediate and unhappy aftermath of the breakdown of her marriage, when she'd been stupid enough to think that having sex would provide some sort of comfort. But it had only taken one unfortunate encounter for her to realise that was a total fallacy. So, it was no good getting too starry-eyed. She might regard last night as a totally magical experience. But, as far as Matt was concerned, it might well have proved to be nothing more than a very pleasant diversion.

'Here, let me dry your fingers,' he murmured, walking across the kitchen and firmly wiping her hands with a thick kitchen towel, before placing his arms about her nervous figure.

'Now…I think it's about time I had a good-morning kiss, don't you?' he continued, before pressing his lips to hers.

The sweetness and warmth of his mouth was wonderfully reassuring, and she savoured the strength of the arms clasping her to the dark hair of his bare chest; her nostrils filled with the cool, astringent scent of his aftershave.

'Incidentally...' he murmured, slowly raising his dark head and regarding her with a faintly quizzical gleam in his green eyes. '*Just* in case you have any doubts about my intentions...I meant everything I said last night.'

'Really?'

'Really and truly—cross my heart and hope to die!' he murmured, both of them smiling at his use of the solemn childhood vow.

'I'm not going to beat about the bush, Sam. We're both sensible adults, and I'm sure you must recognise, as well as I do, that what we have going between us is something very special. And, yes, I know that I hurt you very badly in the past,' he added as she stirred restlessly in his arms. 'But I had no choice. Not with the university authorities breathing down my neck. Not to mention the obvious fact that you were so young—with the whole world in front of you. Believe me, there was no way we could continue our affair.'

'Yes...I can see that now. Although, at the time...'

'At the time, I behaved like a callous brute,' he admitted sadly, his lips tightening in self-disgust as he glimpsed the brief flicker of recollection and pain in her blue eyes.

'But it's all quite different now. We have to let go of the past, because just about everything has changed,' he continued. 'Everything, that is, except our *very* strong attraction for one another. We're both now fully grown up, and although we lead frantically busy lives—we can do it. We *can* make our affair work this time round. In fact, since it only takes four hours to cross the Atlantic by Concorde, I'm going to make *damn certain* that it does work!'

As she gazed up into the deeply hooded green eyes staring down at her so intently, Samantha realised that if she hadn't yet quite managed to sort out all her emotional feelings for this man he was quite right about letting go of the past.

After all, she was a lot older and wiser. There was no way he could ever hurt her again—or cause her to suffer those agonising pangs of first love. All that was water under the bridge. Besides, he'd made it crystal-clear that he was talking about an affair—which meant no total commitment on either side.

You can handle it, she told herself firmly. You're a modern woman, and fully in charge of your emotions, nowadays. Besides, as he'd said, they both had very busy careers.

Making love with Matt was truly wonderful, stupendous—and just about any other glowing adjective she could think of—but it *was* only one part of her life. Her career was vitally important to her, and she wasn't about to give it up for *any* man—even if he was the sexiest thing on two legs!

So, what was there to worry about? She certainly wasn't going to make the mistake of once again falling deeply, irrevocably in love with this man. To be blunt, she'd been there, done that—and worn the T-shirt! Lust was one thing—love quite another. So, there was no reason why she shouldn't have a super-charged, highly intense affair with Matt. Absolutely no reason at all.

'Well…?' Matt demanded tersely, his arms tightening involuntarily about her. 'For heaven's sake, darling—I'm not exactly talking about a fate worse than death! I merely want to make love to you, as often as possible. Surely you're not going to turn me down?'

'Well…I don't seem to have any problem with your basic proposition,' she teased, laughing as he gave a highly dramatic sigh of relief, before once more pressing his lips firmly to hers.

'And now, having sorted out the small print in the contract, I'm going to jump into some casual clothes, and then make us a strong cup of coffee. OK?'

'Ah—*now* you're talking! That's definitely one proposition I'd *never* turn down.' She grinned, suddenly feeling incredibly cheerful and happy.

'Mmm…that was great,' she sighed some time later, having been served toast and marmalade as well as several steaming cups of coffee. 'However, I really can't stay here all day. So, I guess it's time I went back to my hotel.'

'Come along—there's something I want to show you before you go,' he said, rising from the kitchen table. And, although she was disappointed that he hadn't suggested they spend the day together, Samantha had enough sense to realise that without prior knowledge of her visit he undoubtedly had other engagements booked for that day.

'I want you to see why I originally decided to buy this apartment,' he told her, taking her arm and leading her down the hall to the over-decorated sitting room. Operating the remote control to open the curtains, he beckoned her towards the tall, floor-to-ceiling arched windows, which opened on to a small, ornate iron balcony.

'Oh, Matt—it's great! What a wonderful view!' she exclaimed, gazing down at the wide, shady street between his building and the green grass of a large park—which contained a rather grand-looking monument supported on marble columns—and beyond which lay the sparkling blue water of what, she quickly realised, must be the Hudson River. 'Did you spend ages looking at various apartments before finding this one?'

'Well, it did take a long time, and then…'

Whatever else Matt might have been going to say was lost as he was interrupted by the loud, strident tones of the front-door bell.

'Back in a moment,' he muttered, leaving her to admire the view as he walked quickly back across the room towards the hall.

Savouring the early sunshine and bright, fresh morning air, she was only dimly aware of a low buzz of conversation as Matt appeared to be talking to somebody, out in the hall. However, he was soon back by her side, and asking whether she felt like another cup of coffee.

'That would be very nice. But I think I really ought to return to my hotel.'

'Have you got anything in particular lined up for the rest of your stay?'

She shrugged. 'Well, no, not really—but I'd like to see as much of the city as I can. Which is why I must get back, and...'

'I was hoping that you hadn't any firm commitments.' Matt grinned down at her. 'Which is why I've been putting together an itinerary, for the rest of the weekend. And, since you'll be staying here, of course, I think we'd better get dressed and hit the town, as soon as possible.'

She frowned up at him. 'What do you mean, I'm "staying here"? You can't seriously imagine that I'd be prepared to go sightseeing in either this towelling robe or the dress I wore last night? If so, you must be off your trolley!'

'Don't be ridiculous, darling!' he drawled coolly, his deeply hooded green eyes glinting with laughter. 'I wouldn't *dream* of asking you to do any such thing. Which is precisely why I telephoned your hotel, earlier this morning—while you were busy experimenting with the ice-making machine—and asked to have your bags delivered here, to the apartment.'

'*What?* I don't believe it! Are you seriously trying to tell me that you had the nerve to ring my hotel, and...?' She paused, the full enormity of what he'd done suddenly striking home. 'Oh, Lord—you must have got them to pack my suitcases, as well!'

'Certainly I did,' he agreed, with another maddening, cool smile. 'Why would you want to waste a precious hour or two of our valuable time together in such a mundane task?'

'But...but you just can't *do* that sort of thing!' she retorted crossly, appalled to think that some chambermaid had been forced to collect up all her things, empty her drawers and pack her suitcase. Thank goodness she had at least left her bedroom looking reasonably tidy.

But the whole affair was still highly embarrassing. Goodness knows what the hotel must have thought! And what gave Matt the right to act in such a dictatorial, domineering and high-handed manner?

'It's no good telling me I can't do something—especially when it's clearly obvious that I've already done so,' he drawled. The maddening truth of what he was saying only increased her annoyance.

'But I haven't settled the bill, or...'

He waved a dismissive hand. 'That's all been taken care of.'

'Well, thanks a bunch, Matt!' she snapped. 'With my reputation now clearly in shreds, I don't see myself being able to stay at the Mark again. Right?'

'Absolutely right,' he agreed smoothly, placing his arms firmly about her rigid, angry figure. 'Why on earth would you want to stay in a hotel—however comfortable—when you could be curled up in bed with me, here in this apartment?' he added softly, his arms tightening about her as he lowered his dark head.

The sweet seduction of his lips and tongue, together with the close intimate contact with the hard, male contours of his body, was, as usual, proving totally irresistible.

And, after all, Samantha told herself weakly, what was the point of quarrelling over something so unimportant as a suitcase? All that mattered was the fact that his deepening kiss was, as always, causing the blood to race in her veins, her body shivering with delight at the sensual, erotic touch of his fingers as he loosened her robe, slipping his hands inside to caress her warm, naked body.

Trapped in a dense mist of desire and pleasure, she could only give a slight moan as he slowly moved his lips from hers.

'There's no need to be cross with me, sweetheart,' he murmured softly. 'I've merely been putting into practice the agreement we came to, earlier in the kitchen. Which means when you're in New York you stay here with me. Got it?'

She nodded. 'I guess I'm just not used to someone telling me what I can and cannot do. But I'll try to work on it.'

'OK.' Matt grinned. 'Now, I'd like to point out that we have—thanks to my foresight in arranging for your suitcases to be delivered here—managed to save an hour or two of valuable time. Which means,' he added with a low, sensual laugh, 'we can now relax, and go back to bed.'

'You're kidding!'

'Absolutely not,' he drawled blandly, his lips twitching with laughter as he led her firmly back over the thick cream carpet towards the bedroom. 'Surely you must have realised that New York can be a *very* exhausting city?'

'And so we need a rest, right now, to conserve our energies for the day ahead?' she queried ironically, struggling to keep her face straight.

'Precisely!' He paused, turning her around to face him. 'You do, I hope, approve of my new schedule?'

Samantha gazed up at the man who'd so unexpectedly reappeared in her life.

'Well, taking the rough with the smooth...' she began, before giving a muffled laugh as she buried her face in his warm shoulder. 'Yes, my darling Matt, I think I can just about handle it!'

CHAPTER THREE

SAMANTHA paused in the doorway, turning to give a fleeting glance around the huge main living area of her penthouse loft apartment in London.

Her two sisters thought that she was quite mad—particularly the eldest, Edwina, living in cheerful disorder in Gloucestershire with her doctor husband and two noisy, rumbustious young daughters.

However, Samantha had always had an absolute fetish about making sure that her apartment was in pristine, apple-pie order when she left for work in the mornings. Mainly because, when she returned home after a long and exhausting day at the office, she'd found that she needed to relax in a calm, tranquil space which was completely uncluttered.

Now, as always, she got a good deal of satisfaction and enormous pleasure from the sight of the pale oak floorboards and the simply draped, white muslin curtains over the large floor-to-ceiling windows. The current vogue for 'minimalism'—which seemed to involve having as little furniture as possible, with everything tidied away in vast storage cupboards hidden from view—was her idea of absolute heaven.

'But it's so terribly *bare*!' her older sister had shrieked in dismay on her first visit to Samantha's new apartment two years ago.

Shuddering as she'd viewed what seemed blank, empty acres of floor space—broken only by two, huge modern sofas and a deep leather chair, surrounding a long glass and stainless-steel coffee table—Edwina had turned to gaze at her with a worried frown.

'I simply can't believe that you *really* want to live in this great barn of a place? Quite honestly, Sam, it would drive me absolutely up the wall!'

But when Samantha had pointed out to her older sister that this was really what she wanted, Edwina had merely responded with a bewildered shrug of her shoulders. In fact, she had firmly placed the blame for her younger sister's strange taste in interior decoration on a legacy from their Swedish grandmother.

'Well, it *has* to be the answer, Sam. After all, you're the only one of us who inherited Granny's dead straight, pale flaxen hair.

'Yes, I know...' she'd added impatiently as Samantha had rolled her eyes up at the ceiling. 'I know you probably only remember Granny as a white-haired old lady. But I've seen a photograph of her as a young girl—and it could easily have been a picture of you!

'And besides,' Edwina had continued with a laugh, 'I reckon this place would definitely go down a storm in Gothenburg! However, if it's what you really want—then I hope you'll be very happy living here.'

And, indeed, she *had* been extremely happy, Samantha thought, closing her front door and taking the lift down to the ground floor, where her early morning taxi was waiting to take her to the office.

Traffic congestion in the city of London was now so bad that, as Samantha frequently told her friends, anyone who tried to drive to work clearly needed their head examined. Her apartment was situated in the up-and-coming district of Clerkenwell—only a short distance away from her office near St Paul's Cathedral. So, it obviously made sense to leave her car safely parked in the underground car park, beneath her apartment, and take taxis to and from the office.

'G'morning, Miss Thomas,' her regular taxi driver called out as she climbed into the back of the black cab. 'I reckon it's going to be a lovely hot day. In fact, my

wife thinks that it's going to be a real case of flaming
June!'

'You may be right, Joe,' Samantha murmured, extracting a file from her briefcase.

She generally found that this journey to work was a
perfect time to make notes, or jot down any memos concerning the day's work which lay ahead. But this morning, for some unaccountable reason, she didn't seem to
be able to concentrate on business.

Leaning back on the leather seat, she closed her eyes,
trying to ignore the strange nauseous feeling in her stomach.

It was all the fault of that heavy, indigestible meal
which she'd had last night, Samantha told herself ruefully.
It had proved to be virtually impossible to refuse to eat
the dishes, proudly produced by a newly married friend—
who obviously needed to take an urgent course in basic,
everyday cooking!

All of which clearly explained why she was feeling a
bit rough this morning. But goodness—what a contrast to
the wonderful food she'd had at the Four Seasons in New
York, just six weeks ago.

She could feel a hot, crimson flush sweeping up over
her pale cheeks at the memory of that lost weekend. A
weekend when, to her astonishment, she'd seemed to
completely forget all about plain, ordinary everyday life,
and had completely abandoned herself to...to...
Samantha paused in her thoughts, hunting for the right
word to describe accurately what had happened, before
giving a helpless shrug.

Unfortunately, there simply *was* no word which embodied all the extraordinary feelings and sensations which
had so quickly swamped both her mind and body. And,
however shocking it might be to admit the fact, there was
no doubt that she *had* totally abandoned herself to the
overwhelming power...of lust!

In fact, swiftly losing all track of time and space, she

couldn't remember a time of such intense, magical joy and happiness—all crammed into two short days.

After spending that early Saturday morning making thrilling and exciting love to one other, Samantha would have been quite happy either to sit dozing and reading by the fire, or go for a slow, leisurely walk down Riverside Drive, the broad, shady street outside Matt's apartment. However, he had planned quite a different, and far more exhausting, itinerary.

'Come on, lazy bones! Hurry up and get dressed. We've got a lot to do—and very little time in which to do it,' Matt had declared, practically booting her out of bed and into the shower, before transporting her off to Bloomingdale's massive shoe department.

'You're going to be doing a lot of walking. So, buying some flat comfortable shoes has to be the first item on the list,' he'd announced firmly. And then, after insisting on paying for an expensive pair of Ralph Lauren loafers, he'd instructed his chauffeur to drop them outside an enormous and very grand mansion just off Fifth Avenue.

Leading her up the stone steps towards the arched portico, Matt had explained that the priceless art collection of steel magnate Henry Frick was displayed as if he were still alive and living in his old home, providing a rare glimpse of how the extremely wealthy had lived in New York during the Victorian era.

'This city isn't just a mass of business skyscrapers,' he told her as they had a whistle-stop tour past wonderful paintings by Constable, Turner and Jan Vermeer. 'New York has a very definite history all of its own, and I want you to see as much of it as possible.'

And he certainly did his best! In fact, by the time he'd given her a lightning tour of the Whitney Museum of American Art, the Guggenheim Museum, the National Academy of Design and Cooper-Hewitt Museum, Samantha was suffering from a bad case of mental indigestion—and very *sore* feet!

'I've had it!' she told Matt firmly. 'Quite honestly, I don't think I can face seeing another museum. Well, not for the next ten years, anyway,' she added with a wry laugh. 'It's been really great. But now can we *please* go back to your apartment?'

'You've done rather better than I expected,' he admitted with a grin. 'And it might be a good idea to take a breather. Because we've got a heavy schedule for the rest of the day.'

Almost groaning out loud at the thought of what might lie ahead, she was pleased to discover that Matt had only been teasing.

Goodness knows how he'd managed to obtain two tickets for *La Bohème* at the Metropolitan Opera House. But she was thrilled by the performance, and was still wiping a stray tear from her eyes over the tragic death of poor Mimi when she found herself being escorted into the Café Des Artistes.

'I thought this place might cheer you up,' he told her as they were led to their table. And, indeed, the boisterous, jolly café with its 1930s murals of frolicking nymphs proved to be an amazingly light-hearted place.

And so it went on. Another night of wonderful love-making, followed by yet another walk!

However, strolling through Greenwich Village on a Sunday morning proved to be a far more relaxing experience than the previous day's frantic dash through New York's premier museums. Eating sticky pastries at Caffè Vivaldi and viewing a beautiful row of Italianate houses, before ambling slowly through Washington Square, made it a day to remember. And in the evening, after returning home to Matt's apartment, she was delighted to find that he'd arranged to have a romantic dinner delivered to his door, enabling them to have a last, quiet evening together.

'It's been a wonderful two days,' she told him, slowly putting down her empty coffee cup at the end of the meal. 'It's going to be very hard…because…well, there's no point in pretending that I'm not feeling very, very sad about having to fly back to London tomorrow.'

'It won't be for long, darling,' he said, firmly clasping her hand in his and raising it to his lips. 'You know I'm crazy about you. So, I'll be seeing as much of you as I can. As I said yesterday, it only takes four hours to cross the Atlantic Ocean by Concorde. Besides, I'm hoping that it's going to be a two-way traffic. So, if you should just happen to find you have a free weekend, you can hop on a plane to New York. Which is why,' he added with a grin, handing her a long white envelope, 'I thought you might find this useful.'

'Oh, *Matt*!' she exclaimed, gazing down in amazement at a letter from a well-known travel agency, with offices in London and New York, confirming that they would provide an unlimited number of first-class or Concorde airline tickets to Miss Samantha Thomas—for travel on any date during the coming year. 'I really don't know what to say!' She looked at him helplessly. 'It's *very* generous of you. But there was no need...I mean, travelling in that style is so utterly and horrendously expensive, and...'

'Nonsense!' Matt waved a dismissive hand. 'The whole point of the exercise is that I'm determined to have you in my bed—as often as possible!' He grinned. 'After all, what's money for—if not to buy the things that one *really* wants and desires? And, believe me, my darling,' he added with a husky laugh, 'I most definitely want and desire you!

'Obviously we can't abandon our own two, individual lives at the drop of a hat,' he continued. 'But when I said that, having found each other once again, we *can* make it work this time—I meant every word. In any case, quite apart from being lovers, we've had a lot of fun together. Haven't we?'

Samantha smiled at him. 'Yes, you're quite right. It

really has been great fun—even if my feet are still aching from that mad dash around the museums!'

'There will be problems from time to time, of course,' he told her with a shrug. 'Principally because we're both such busy people—with hectic jobs and often an exhausting schedule of work to get through. But nothing that we can't handle, right?'

Yes, once again Matt was quite right, Samantha told herself. They'd had a lot of fun together. And, while she realised that, like all good things, it was now coming to an end with her flight back to England tomorrow, she felt comforted by the thought that they would see each other again, very soon. As for her ability to 'handle' their semi-detached love affair? All her original fears and trepidation about becoming involved once again with this man seemed quite ridiculous, if not totally absurd.

But now, as the congested traffic brought her taxi to a sudden, juddering halt, Samantha wasn't quite so sure that she was absolutely, one hundred per cent in charge of her emotions.

Because what had actually happened, following Matt's avowed intention to see her as often as possible? *Nada*...zilch...absolutely *nothing*!

Despite knowing that she was being totally unreasonable, she was becoming increasingly fed up at only receiving tantalising short phone calls, or brief, highly unsatisfactory messages—even if they were attached to large bouquets of flowers—from Matt, who, for the past month, seemed to have been travelling non-stop around the globe. All of which meant that their love affair wasn't just 'semi-detached'—it was virtually non-existent.

Oh, come on—get a grip! And stop behaving like a neurotic teenager, she told herself roughly, simply not able to understand why she should be suffering from such acute, emotional mood swings as she had during the past week. One moment it seemed as though she was dreaming about their lovemaking—utterly frustrated as she lay alone in her bed, wanting him like crazy. And then, a few moments later, she'd find herself full of doom and gloom, convinced that the whole idea of a love affair with Matt was totally ridiculous—and not even sure that she wanted to see him again.

However, the worrying factor, as far as she was concerned, was the simple fact that she really *was* spending far too much time thinking about Matthew Warner. Which was damn silly.

Most men of her acquaintance were easily capable of keeping their private and business lives quite separate—mentally closing a door in their mind when they went off to work, and opening it again when they returned home. So, why was she having such a problem? Why did she—who normally had no trouble concentrating on the job in hand—now find her work disturbed by visions of Matt's dark, handsome face? Or spend time daydreaming about the time they'd spent together in New York, when she should have been fully absorbed by a company balance sheet?

However, if her private life seemed highly unsatisfactory—and her brief affair with Matt almost over before it had ever really begun—she still found her job a particularly busy and fulfilling one. So, clearly it was time that she devoted more attention to the development of her business career.

As if on cue, and just as she had finished giving herself such good, prudent and wise advice, the taxi came to a halt outside a large modern office block.

After entering the building and taking the elevator up to the fourth floor, she was surprised as she walked down the corridor leading to her office to find some of her young business partners huddled in a group, whispering urgently to each other.

'Hi—what's up?' she asked as her assistant, Henry Graham, followed her into her office.

'Paul Unwin has gone.'

'What?' Samantha frowned, spinning around to face him. 'What on earth are you talking about?'

Henry shrugged. 'Apparently, Paul handed in his notice late on Friday night, after we'd all gone home.'

'You're joking!'

'No.' Henry shook his head. 'There's a strong rumour that he's been head-hunted to join all those new guys at Paramount Asset Management. But nobody knows for certain.'

'Good heavens!'

Samantha sank down into the chair behind her desk, stunned by the news of the sudden departure of the head of their department, Paul Unwin. 'Are you *absolutely* certain about this?'

'Well, we haven't had the "official" news from the powers that be on the top floor,' Henry told her, with another shrug of his broad shoulders. 'However, there have already been one or two calls from reporters, asking whether we can confirm the rumours about Paul joining P.A.M. So, I reckon it must be kosher, don't you?'

'I suppose so,' she muttered, still not quite able to believe that her boss had departed, so suddenly, for pastures new.

'What's going to happen to the department?'

'There's no point in asking me,' she told him, opening her briefcase and extracting some files, before adding wryly, 'After all—I only work here. Right?'

Henry waved an elegant, dismissive hand. 'I meant…who do you think is going to be promoted to Paul's job?'

'How the hell would I know?' Samantha snapped, before taking a deep breath and giving him a slight smile of apology.

'I'm sorry. I'm just a bit shaken by the news, that's all. However, as far as Paul's job is concerned, it's far too early to think about something like that. In any case,' she added dismissively, 'I reckon that they could well bring in somebody from outside.'

'They might...' Henry murmured doubtfully. 'But I reckon it's a lot more likely that the management will promote someone from within the department. In fact—' he gave her a wide grin '—I reckon I could have some fun running a sweepstake on just *who* will get the job. What do you think?'

'Oh, for heaven's sake, Henry!' Samantha sighed, wondering—not for the first time—what on earth she'd done to deserve being burdened with the Honourable Henry Graham.

The eldest son of an aristocratic father, who also just happened to be one of the directors of Minerva Utilities Management, Henry had a bad track record in the past, as far as gainful employment was concerned. Which was clearly a pity, since at first sight he would appear to have everything going for him.

Approximately her own age, Henry was tall and always extremely well dressed, with dark gold hair brushed back from an extraordinarily handsome face. He possessed great charm, an infectious laugh, and was extremely easygoing. But, oh Lord, was he dim or what? Just about as thick as two planks of wood!

In fact, if there *was* anything in that handsome head of his—other than an extensive, encyclopaedic knowledge of London high society—Samantha had yet to discover it!

As Henry was the son of one of her firm's directors, and also appeared regularly in the social columns of the tabloid newspapers, she'd had a good idea of the problems which might lie ahead when she'd been called into the office of her boss, Paul Unwin, six months ago.

'Oh, no!' Samantha had groaned, on being informed that Henry Graham had been appointed as her new assistant, and was due to start work the following week.

'Come on, Paul—give me a break?' she'd begged. 'I

need someone like Dopey Henry about as much as I need a hole in the head! Can't you allocate him to someone else?'

'I'm sorry, Sam,' he'd shrugged, before explaining that it was the head of the company who had made the decision.

'Apparently, our chairman thinks that you're the only one likely to be tough enough to cope with the rich, idle layabout. Which I suppose, when you think about it,' Paul had added reflectively, 'is really quite a compliment.'

'Oh, yeah? Well, I'm not exactly thrilled to hear that the chairman views me as a "tough" woman. So, I reckon it's a compliment I can do without,' she'd told him with a hollow laugh, before glumly trudging back to her own office.

In fact, rather surprisingly, she and Henry had managed to get on reasonably well. Just as long as she double-checked everything he did—and never made the mistake of expecting him to finish even the smallest job on time—he'd proved to be extremely good company.

An unexpected development had been the fact that, for some strange reason, Henry had also developed a bit of a crush on her.

However, after making it crystal-clear that she *never*, under any circumstances, mixed business and pleasure, Samantha had to admit that it was very nice to receive so many bouquets of exotic flowers. And she wasn't averse to accepting his invitations to dine at very glamorous, if hideously expensive restaurants occasionally.

But now, as she handed him a report which she'd prepared over the weekend—asking him to check the figures and let her have it back later on, that afternoon—Samantha knew that she'd be lucky if she saw that piece of paper again before next weekend.

Because, knowing Henry, he'd undoubtedly be spending his time more profitably, and having a lot more fun, by running a sweepstake on who would get her old boss's job.

And she was absolutely right. Throughout the rest of the week, despite trying to concentrate on the work in hand, she was constantly disturbed by Henry popping into her office and quoting the latest odds on who was likely to get the position.

'Everyone seems to think that Alistair is going to land the job,' he'd told her only yesterday, referring to a newly married and slightly older colleague who'd been with the firm for some time.

'Well…why not? He'd be a good choice,' she had muttered, far too busy to be bothered with her assistant's current preoccupation with the betting odds in the office sweepstake.

'You could be right, I suppose. Unfortunately, Alistair sort of lacks any charisma, if you know what I mean?'

'Yes, I *do* happen to know what the word means—which I guess is more than you do!' she'd retorted. 'Now, for goodness' sake, go and get on with some work. Incidentally, have you organised the purchase of those investment bonds yet?'

But it was like talking to a deaf child. Henry clearly wasn't interested in anything as boring as investment bonds—not when he could spend his time more enjoyably, and with the prospect of making some easy money.

'Actually,' he'd said slowly, 'I reckon the really *smart* money would go on a bright, long shot—like yourself.'

'Oh, for heaven's sake! If you're as successful at betting as you are at investment, I reckon that you're going to lose your shirt, Henry,' she'd retorted crossly. 'Now, go away. I don't want to hear any more of this nonsense.'

'Well, I reckon I *am* going to put my money on you, Sam. Nobody seems to think you've got a chance, of course. Which means that if you *do* get the promotion I'm going to scoop the pool!'

'OK, Henry—that's it! It's time for you to get a

life…get lost—and, above all, get the hell out of my office. *Right this minute!*' she'd yelled, thoroughly fed up
to the back teeth with all his nonsense.

However, she wasn't an idiot. She was well aware that
quite a few of her fellow workers had been manoeuvring,
and networking like mad, in the hope of obtaining Paul
Unwin's job.

Well—there you go. That was life in the fast lane, in
the City of London, she told herself that evening, feeling
tired and weary at the end of a long, hard working day
as she let herself into her apartment.

Although she was technically in the running for her old
boss's position, Samantha saw no point in bothering to
get involved in any of the ongoing intrigues.

Quite apart from anything else, she was quite certain
that the senior directors and chairman of her firm were
more than capable of making up their own minds about
who should get the job. And to be seen as too ruthlessly
ambitious might well prove counter-productive. Besides
which, even if she had felt inclined to canvass support for
herself, she was actually far too busy to find the time to
do so. And if that meant Henry losing his shirt, by placing
his money on the wrong horse, that was just his bad luck!

As always, the peace and serenity of her surroundings
did much to soothe her tired mind and body. Entering the
main room, she automatically checked her telephone answering machine, remembering to set it to audio call-
screening—for single ladies, living alone, the most sensible way of not taking unwanted calls—before going
through into the kitchen to make herself a cool drink.

After preparing a quick supper, and sitting out up on
her roof terrace, enjoying the sight of so many wonderful
old buildings spread out in a panorama before her,
Samantha suddenly realised that she hadn't bought a card
to accompany her niece's birthday present. Since she was
due to visit her sister's family in Gloucestershire that
weekend, it would be black marks all round if the pres-

ent—a fluffy white ballet skirt—wasn't accompanied by a suitable card.

Unfortunately, after hunting in vain through various drawers for a spare birthday card, Samantha drew a blank.

Oh, well—it would be easy enough to buy one tomorrow, in her lunch hour, she was just telling herself as she tidied all the papers and cards back into the drawer, when a small photograph fluttered down onto the floor.

'Good Lord! Didn't we look awful?' she muttered to herself, walking slowly across the room, before sinking down into a wide leather chair and holding the black and white photograph under the light of a nearby lamp.

It was almost bizarre how much fashions had changed in the last eight or nine years. Because there she was, with two of her best friends at university, all dressed up for an evening out on the town—and thinking they looked the cat's pyjamas! She still saw a lot of Philippa, of course, but what on earth had happened to Marie?

Marie Holden had been easily the brightest of the students studying economics, and it was strange that Samantha hadn't heard the other girl's name mentioned as a high-flyer in the City before now. And, of course, with the clear-minded logic which she'd brought to bear on her studies, it had been Marie who'd pointed out to Samantha, all those years ago, that she was playing with fire.

'Going out with a professor is bad news. Being stupid enough to fall in love with him is a disaster!' Marie had told her bluntly.

But, of course, she hadn't listened to such sage advice, had she?

Leaning back in her chair, Samantha recalled just how dazed she'd been at having attracted the attention of her tall, handsome tutor. And equally thrilled to know that she was the envy of all her friends.

It had been the start of her third year at university and, naturally, she'd had several semi-serious boyfriends and one or two mad infatuations for highly unsuitable men. However, as the days had passed and their relationship had progressed, she'd known that she was, for the very first time in her life, deeply and truly in love.

Totally deaf to all advice, utterly blind to the harsh realities of life, she'd had absolutely no doubt that what she felt for that tall, dark, highly intelligent and clever man, Matthew Warner, was absolutely the *real thing*. And, when he'd suggested spending a weekend in a small inn by the river in Minster Lovell—sufficiently far enough away from Oxford, to enable them to escape detection—she'd been so desperately in love that she'd have willingly followed him to the ends of the earth, if necessary.

The inn itself had been a delight. And, as they'd walked down by the river in the late autumn evening, before dinner, the night air heavy with the aromatic smell of wood smoke and damp greenery, Samantha had known that she had never, ever been so deliriously happy in all her young life.

Nor had she ever been able to forget their first nights of passion in the large, four-poster bed—the softly soothing yet arousing touch of his hands on her body, the mastery with which he'd led her gently from one erotic sensation to another, until she had truly thought she would die of ecstasy.

It had seemed to her young and still very inexperienced mind and body that he somehow possessed an extraordinary ability to carry her far beyond the universe, to the stars and on to infinity, where nothing existed but fierce waves of both unimaginable and totally unexplainable pleasure. Pleasure that spiralled and exploded into a myriad of shooting stars, before leaving her to free-fall back through the stratosphere, gliding slowly back down to earth, and into a deep sleep, held closely within his warm embrace.

As the weeks had passed, and because liaisons between

lecturers and their students were obviously frowned upon by the university authorities, they'd been forced to be circumspect and careful about where and when they met to make love. And that, she could see now, had merely added an extra, thrilling spice and excitement to their affair—an affair which, if she had only known it, was clearly doomed from the start.

Totally gripped by an emotional intensity that hitherto she'd only found in books or poetry, she had undoubtedly been intoxicatingly in love, with love itself—and existing in a fool's paradise.

Samantha was older and wiser now, of course. And she couldn't reasonably blame Matt for taking the hard, tough decision to end their affair. Especially as she would never have found the strength to do so herself.

It had all happened on one cold Sunday winter's afternoon when, after they'd been making slow, delicious love by the roaring log fire in the small house which he rented during term time, Matt had broken the dreadful news.

'But you *can't* mean it? You can't possibly mean that we're never to see each other, ever again?' she'd cried, totally unable to believe what he was saying. 'Not...not just after having made love to me...?''

'I couldn't help myself,' he'd sighed heavily, a deep flush rising over his cheeks. 'I know it was wrong. But I couldn't resist...not just one more time...' His voice, heavy with self-disgust, had trailed away into silence.

'But *why*?' she'd demanded hysterically. And, even when he'd patiently explained, time and again, that, rumours having come to the ears of his superiors, both his job and her future career were now in jeopardy, she *still* hadn't been able to grasp fully what was happening to her.

Totally devastated by his rejection, she'd virtually withdrawn from university life. It had only been the kindness and patience of her friends and family, together with the caring support of her old friend, the artist Alan

Gifford—who'd seemed happily prepared to allow her to weep copious tears on his thin, bony shoulders—that had enabled her to complete her studies and, against all the odds, obtain a good degree. And, when Alan had declared that he wanted to marry her, Samantha, who at that point hadn't much cared *what* she did, had apathetically agreed that, yes, maybe it was a good idea.

Samantha gave a sigh, putting down the photograph and leaning back in her chair. Poor Alan. There had never been any chance that he and she would live happily ever after. And there had been nothing that either of them could do about it. Not when she'd still been so madly in love with Matt.

However, the passage of time had, as always, blunted the pain of that unhappy love affair. When she and Alan Gifford had finally called it a day, Samantha had known that the break-up of her marriage had been mostly her fault. Which was one of the reasons why she had never blamed him in any way, and why she'd made a considerable effort always to keep in touch, and remain good friends with her ex-husband.

The distant sound of a church clock chiming the hour brought her sharply back down to earth—together with the realisation that there was no point in sitting here, indulging in sad memories.

Her marriage to Alan was now something that she must consign to the past, together with her unhappy memories of that feverish, brief first love affair with Matt. Although if she didn't get herself off to bed right away she might well not have much of a future, she told herself grimly. Because the prime requisites for a successful fund manager were robust good health and steady nerves—both qualities relying heavily on a good night's sleep.

But, as her stomach gave another of the weird, strange lurches which she'd been suffering from lately, she decided that it probably *was* time she saw a doctor.

Maybe it was her nervous system acting up for some

reason? Or possibly she was suffering with some strange form of summer flu. But, whatever the cause, she couldn't go on feeling slightly sick most of the time. Especially not at this stage of her career, when she had more than enough work to get through each day, without the additional burden of not being in good health.

Busy at work the next day, Samantha forgot all about her intention of seeing a doctor until, following a hurried lunch at a small, local city restaurant, she once again experienced that slightly nauseous feeling in her stomach.

Back at her desk, she took out her address book, and was just about to lift the phone, to call her doctor for an appointment, when the instrument gave a sharp ring.

Lifting the receiver, all she could hear was a loud crackling in her ears, followed by a distant roaring sound, but no trace of a human voice.

'Oh, for heaven's sake,' she muttered, replacing the phone. Immediately she'd done so, it rang again.

Muttering under her breath, she picked it up for the second time.

'Hello, darling...' A faint voice broke through the crackling background.

'*Matt!* Is that really you?' she shouted, not one hundred per cent certain that it *was* him at the other end of the line.

'Relax; there's no need to yell!' Matt's voice was very clear as the background atmospherics suddenly disappeared. 'I'm sorry not to have been in touch for a while, darling. I've been heavily involved with a lot of business problems.'

'Where exactly are you, at the moment?'

'Well, let's see...' He gave a low chuckle of laughter. 'I *think* I've still got a toe-hold in the Far East. But I'm catching a plane in an hour's time to Zurich—and I should be landing at London, Heathrow, late Friday afternoon. So, at least we'll be able to spend some time together. OK?'

'Oh, Matt—that's wonderful!' she gasped breathlessly, all her doubts and fears that he might have had second thoughts, and decided that their love affair wasn't such a good idea after all, vanishing into thin air. And then she suddenly remembered a pressing engagement.

'But…but I *can't* make next weekend,' she cried, her high spirits plummeting into the depths of despair. 'I've simply got to go down to Gloucestershire. It's Rosie's birthday party.'

'Who on earth is Rosie?' he ground out, his sudden flash of anger clearly audible down the line.

Samantha gave a heavy sigh. 'She's my niece, the youngest of my older sister's two daughters—and I'm her godmother as well as her aunt. I haven't been down to see the family for simply ages. So, I gave my word that I'd definitely be there, this coming weekend. I…I simply *can't* get out of it,' she wailed.

'Hey, relax, sweetheart,' Matt said. 'There's no reason why I can't come too, is there?'

'What…?' she muttered, playing for time, her mind racing at a speed of knots as she tried to work out all the angles raised by his suggestion. 'You mean…you mean come down with me, and stay the night with my sister, in Gloucestershire?'

'Yes, why ever not?'

'Well…' She hesitated, easily able to think of at least half a dozen reasons why it would *not* be a good idea for him to accompany her to her sister's house in the country at the weekend.

For one thing, she didn't know exactly what he felt for her. Nor was she entirely certain of her feelings for him. And, knowing her older sister as well as she did, there was always the ghastly chance of Edwina deciding that Matt was the best thing since sliced bread—and indulging in a mad bout of matchmaking. Or, possibly even worse, taking an instant dislike to him, and treating Matt with arctic coldness and freezing him out of the family. Besides, she didn't want her sisters to feel sorry for her if her new love affair—which had hardly begun—suddenly went down the tubes.

'Come on, Sam…what's the problem?'

'There's no problem, Matt. It's just that…' She paused, suddenly going hot and cold as she realised how she'd lied about her marriage. Why, oh, *why* hadn't she told him the truth, that night in the Four Seasons restaurant, in New York? On top of which, her younger sister, Georgie—who'd never been known to keep her mouth shut about anything—was almost certainly bound to let the cat out of the bag.

'Sweetheart, this is ridiculous.' His impatient sigh was clearly audible down the phone. 'Do you or do you not want to see me?'

'Yes…yes, of course I do!' she assured him.

'But you don't want me to meet your family? Or your sister can't cope with unexpected guests? Or you've got some other boyfriend turning up, and things could get just a little awkward? He gave a sardonic laugh. 'I hope it's not the last one, Sam?'

'No, of course it's not,' she retorted firmly, quickly deciding, *What the hell?* Yes, she'd be taking a risk, but 'risk management' was what she dealt with every day of the week. Right? And if the whole visit went pear-shaped, well…that was life.

'I was just…well, the thing is, Matt, I couldn't quite see you in the midst of a whole mass of seven-year-olds, singing "Happy Birthday" along with the rest of us,' she muttered, ashamed of telling a very small white lie. 'But if you feel strong enough to hack it, then of course I know my sister would be very pleased to see you.'

Matt laughed. 'Relax, sweetheart. I'm a dab hand at birthday parties,' he told her, before giving the flight number and time of his arrival from Zurich. 'See you on

Friday,' he said, then there was a click and the phone went dead.

With a heavy sigh, Samantha slowly replaced the receiver. It wasn't that she didn't want to see Matt—because, of course, she could hardly wait. But how he would react to her older sister's chaotic household she had absolutely no idea.

Besides, he wouldn't just be meeting Edwina, her husband David, who was a busy doctor, and their two young daughters. There was also the problem of her sister, Georgie.

A feather-brained, dark-blonde-haired girl, with an amazing figure—and someone who *definitely* didn't believe in letting work get in the way of her social life!—Georgie had never been known to think before saying the first thing that came into her head. A real case of foot-in-mouth syndrome which, in the past, had caused untold embarrassment to each and every member of the family.

All of which meant that, quite apart from all her other problems, Samantha could practically guarantee that next weekend was likely to prove to be an absolute disaster!

CHAPTER FOUR

SPOTTING the signpost, Samantha moved into the slow lane of traffic, preparing to turn off the M4 motorway on her way to her sister's home in Gloucestershire.

Luckily, the traffic wasn't too bad, and it was still light enough on a June evening to not yet need her headlights. In fact, after checking the clock dial on her dashboard, she realised that they were likely to arrive slightly earlier than she'd expected.

Briefly turning her head to cast a swift glance at the recumbent figure lying stretched out in the seat beside her, Samantha grinned, before quickly turning her attention back to the road in front of her. Despite his assurance that he never suffered from jet-lag, Matt was now clearly fast asleep!

Heathrow had, as usual, proved to be a real pain—the Friday evening rush-hour traffic and the seemingly never-ending road works clogging the route leading to the airport. However, she'd luckily arranged to leave work early, which meant that she'd had plenty of time to park her car and meet Matt's flight from Switzerland, which had only been delayed by a few minutes.

Prey to massive doubts and feelings of deep insecurity, she'd been overwhelmingly relieved to discover that Matt seemed highly delighted to see her. Clearly every bit as happy as she had been to find herself clasped tightly in his arms—and being given a long, satisfying kiss—to the obvious amusement of his fellow passengers, forced to edge their luggage trolleys around the couple, embracing slap bang in the middle of the entrance to the terminal.

'I've missed you like crazy, but there was nothing I

could do. Because it's been hell on wheels, businesswise, for the past six weeks,' Matt explained as she led him to where she had parked her car. 'Ah—a nice, zippy little roadster. I always did like BMWs,' he added, happily settling down into the passenger seat, and quickly disclaiming any intention of driving the vehicle himself.

'Oh, no—I'm *definitely* not one of those men who refuse to be driven by a woman,' he laughed.

'Besides…' he quickly pulled a lever, lowering his seat to an almost horizontal position '…I'm more than happy to take advantage of being able to relax and stretch out in comfort. So, drive on, James—and kindly don't spare the horses!'

'At least one thing hasn't changed during the past six weeks, O, Mighty One. You're still indulging in pathetic, lousy male fantasies!' She grinned, not able to hide her sheer happiness and joy at being together with Matt once again.

'So, what *has* changed since we last saw one another?' he queried, almost causing her to curse under her breath at her own stupidity. How could she have forgotten that Matt had always been as fast and sharp as a knife?

'Well…?'

'Oh, nothing much,' she murmured, unwilling at this early point in their reunion to confess to having spent so many sleepless nights in desperate longing for this man. A man who, until two days ago, she'd thought might well have walked out of her life for ever.

'Incidentally,' she continued quickly, anxious to turn his attention in a quite different direction, 'I can't understand how or why—when it's obviously part of my job to know *exactly* who's who, in the world of global finance—I managed to miss your appointment as chief executive of Broadwood Securities?

'Well, I was only head-hunted fairly recently,' he explained. 'And, as you probably know, the company had got itself into a hell of a mess.'

'Yes, I did hear about that.'

Matt gave a heavy sigh. 'Unfortunately—and this is definitely not something I'd like you to repeat—the previous chairman and chief executive, despite being given the sack, is refusing to go quietly.'

'Oh, dear!'

Matt gave a caustic laugh. 'I can think of a stronger expression! However, the ex-chairman is stamping around, like an elephant on heat, loudly demanding God knows how much compensation for having his contract terminated so abruptly. All of which means that my appointment has not yet been publicly endorsed by the board of directors.'

'Maniac!' Samantha muttered beneath her breath, momentarily distracted by the threat of a driver just ahead, mobile phone clamped tightly to his ear as he wove dangerously in and out of the stream of traffic.

'All the same,' she added, picking up the thread of their conversation, when it was safe to do so, 'I ought to give myself a black mark for not having heard anything on the City grapevine.'

'It's nothing but a damn rumour factory!' he snapped, before quickly pulling himself together. 'Sorry, sweetheart, but it's the same thing on Wall Street. It's practically impossible to keep any company business private and under wraps, these days.'

'Well…it depends on which way you're looking down the telescope, doesn't it?' she pointed out. '*My* business, for instance, relies very heavily on titbits of gossip, or early news of a company take-over. As you know,' she added with a shrug, 'in our sort of business, switching company pension funds either in or out of stocks and shares, which are likely to go up or down, can make a dramatic difference to funds we look after. And which, at the end of the day, means a better and much higher pension for the ordinary guy in the street.'

Matt gave a heavy sigh, 'Yes, I know. But all that

gossip isn't much help, and can definitely be counter-productive if, say, a large company is trying to put to-gether a complicated deal. Still…' He shrugged his broad shoulders, grinning as he added, 'I guess we'd better agree to differ on that score. So, I guess I'd do better to concentrate on admiring the passing scenery.'

'It's changed,' she warned him. 'There are now far more roads and huge motorways than when you were last living here.'

'Nevertheless, it's great to be back in England, after so many years. I'd forgotten just how beautifully green everything is,' he added with a slight sigh of contentment. 'June is really the perfect time to see the countryside at its very best, isn't it?'

But now, as she glanced again at the man dozing beside her, Samantha wasn't surprised that he had dropped off into a light sleep. Because he was looking a good deal more tired than when she'd last seen him, his face drawn and strained beneath the overlying deep tan which he'd obviously acquired in the Far East.

It was strange how uptight and, at times, how depressed she'd been about her new relationship with this man. Because once she'd first set eyes on him, in the arrivals terminal at Heathrow, all her doubts and fears about the wisdom of embarking on a new love affair with Matt had suddenly disappeared.

Once again, when alone with Matt, everything seemed very simple. They were friends as well as lovers, and despite the unfortunate history lying behind their break-up, all those years ago, when she *was* with him, Samantha had no problem in believing that she could easily cope with a non-emotional love affair. If there ever *can* be such a thing, she reminded herself warily, before giving a slight shake of her head at her own folly.

What on earth was wrong with her these days? As far as her and Matt's relationship was concerned, she seemed to be swinging violently back and forth—one minute thinking that everything in the garden was absolutely wonderful, then, in almost the twinkling of an eye, suddenly finding herself plunged into the deepest gloom.

It was clearly time that she pulled herself together, took a deep breath and calmed down. A touch of *che sarà sarà* would be a good idea at this stage of her love affair with Matt, she told herself firmly. 'What will be, will be' was, in point of fact, the right attitude to take to just about everything in life. And in any case, she reminded herself grimly, she was still going to have to get through the coming weekend.

'OK...here we are, at last,' she announced some time later, rousing Matt with a slight nudge as she turned off a minor country road, driving past a pair of rusty iron gates and down a long, bumpy gravel track.

'Right,' he said, immediately wide awake and alert, as if someone had suddenly thrown a switch and jerked him abruptly into life. A moment later, with a swift adjustment of his seat, he was sitting upright, and gazing with interest at the fields either side of them.

'Is your sister's husband a farmer?'

'No, far from it,' she said, and explained that David Lancaster was a busy local doctor. 'But he and Edwina have always wanted to live deep in the country, with children, dogs, ponies and other various forms of livestock.'

'Sounds a good way of life to me.'

'Hmm...' Samantha murmured doubtfully, not at all sure that she would want to live buried in the country.

'And what about your parents? Do they live nearby?'

Samantha shook her head. 'No. My father was a busy architect, but he and my mother always had itchy feet. So, as soon as their children were grown up, and able to fend for themselves, Dad took early retirement. And now they're spending their days slowly sailing around the world. They miss us and the grandchildren, of course. But they do seem to be having the time of their lives.'

'That sounds great. I almost envy them,' Matt said

slowly. 'The rat race of city life isn't all it's cracked up to be.'

'Too many rats?' she queried, with a straight face, before they both burst into laughter.

'By the way, I might have forgotten to mention the level of noise and general chaos,' she added casually, as if only just recalling an insignificant item—and hadn't deliberately chosen to avoid telling him the bad news for as long as possible.

'There's no need to worry,' he replied, quickly picking up the note of tension in her voice. 'I'm quite sure that I'm going to enjoy myself.'

Let's hope so, Samantha prayed silently as she brought the car to a halt outside the front door of a long, low, half-timbered farmhouse.

As soon as she switched off the engine, they were immediately engulfed by what seemed a chattering crowd of people, packs of wildly barking dogs, and a loudly clacking gaggle of geese.

Ruefully viewing the expression of startled surprise and confusion on Matt's handsome face, she suddenly remembered that he'd been the only child of a widowed mother, who had died during his first year at university. Oh, Lord—this weekend really *was* going to be a baptism of fire for the poor guy!

However, she definitely had to award him an alpha-plus for making a remarkably swift recovery.

Although clearly stunned by all the deafening clamour and hubbub, by the time he'd swung his long legs out of the car Matt had somehow managed to sort out the individual members of the family. Wishing a very happy birthday to Rosie, the youngest of the two children, he reached into the car to open his briefcase, handing a small package to the Birthday Girl, before presenting his hostess, Edwina, with an enormous box of Swiss chocolates.

'Smooth Bastard!' Samantha muttered under her breath, grimly forced to admire the sight of her normally tough, strong-minded older sister immediately succumbing to Matt's overwhelming charm. In fact, if it wasn't such a ridiculous idea, Samantha knew that she'd definitely be wary of someone who possessed such amazing social dexterity, and a seemingly effortless ability to cajole the birds from the trees.

'Oh, Sam—he's simply *gorgeous*!' Edwina exclaimed later as the two sisters chatted together while preparing the evening meal. 'And *so* generous! Rosie is just over the moon about her present. That tiny little silver heart on a silver chain, from Tiffany's, was an absolutely perfect choice.'

Samantha, busy mashing potatoes, turned to smile at her sister. 'Of course, she's still a bit too young to get overly excited about being given one of those exciting sky-blue boxes, tied with white ribbon. But I must admit to being quite envious when I saw its contents.'

'Mmm...so was I. And talking of hearts...' Edwina hesitated for a moment. 'Is it...er...just a casual friendship with Matt?' she probed carefully, obviously dying to know what was going on between Samantha and her amazingly charming boyfriend. 'Or could this be a seriously important relationship?'

'No...well, it's not really like that,' Samantha told her cautiously. 'The thing is...we've only just met up again, after not having seen each other for a long time. So...' she shrugged '...it's anyone's guess how things will turn out.'

'I didn't realise...' Edwina turned around from chopping an onion to look at her sister in surprise. 'Do you mean that Matt is an old boyfriend?'

'Yes...er...I suppose he comes under that heading.'

'But I don't remember having met him before. And quite honestly, Sam, I'm sure that I wouldn't have forgotten anyone *quite* so scrummy!'

The younger girl shrugged. 'It was a very long time ago. When I was at university. And, in any case, I never brought him home to meet Mum and Dad. It wasn't…well, he was quite a lot older than me, and I wasn't sure that they'd approve.'

'Oh, Sam!' Her sister suddenly frowned with concern, recalling the younger girl's first 'grand passion' which had apparently ended so tragically, leaving her devastated and bitterly unhappy for such a long time. 'I never met him, of course. But surely it wasn't *Matt* who caused you all that heartache so long ago?'

'Yes, I'm afraid so,' Samantha agreed with a twisted smile. 'So, you can see why I'm taking things a bit carefully.'

'Does he know about your first marriage?'

Samantha shook her head. 'No…I haven't exactly…er…well, the thing is…I didn't quite tell him the truth,' she muttered, not meeting her sister's eyes as she busied herself shaking water from the lettuce before adding it to the salad bowl. 'In fact…well, I've got to admit that I didn't tell him I *had* been married before,' she added in a rush.

'Oh, dear—that doesn't sound very sensible.'

'I know…I know…' she muttered quickly, feeling her face growing hot as she stared out of the kitchen window, still deliberately keeping her back firmly turned to her sister.

'But it was so difficult,' she continued. 'I mean…there we were, right in the middle of a very glamorous restaurant. And I simply couldn't face going into a long, involved explanation of exactly why I'd made the great mistake of marrying Alan. Quite apart from the fact that I still feel a bit raw about that stupid and disastrous marriage of mine.'

'But I thought you didn't have any feelings for Alan?' Edwina shook her head in confusion. 'Surely it's all over between you?'

'Oh, heavens, yes.' Samantha relaxed, turning around to face her sister. 'We're still reasonably friendly, of course. But that's all,' she explained. 'If anything really worries me, nowadays, it's being such a fool in marrying someone whom I didn't truly love. It still hurts. The fact that I was such an idiot, I mean,' she added hastily.

Edwina shrugged. 'If that's the case, I don't understand why you didn't tell Matt the truth?'

'Because...because I was still madly in love with *him* when I agreed to marry Alan Gifford,' she pointed out, her voice tight with exasperation. 'There was no way I could tell Matt that particular piece of information—not in the middle of a restaurant, when we'd only just met up again after so many years. And most definitely *not* when I wasn't even sure whether he was chatting me up—or what I was going to do about it if he was!'

In the long silence that followed, Samantha bitterly regretted having let her exasperation get the better of her. Why the hell hadn't she kept her mouth shut?

'For goodness' sake—please don't tell anyone else. I couldn't face...'

'Don't worry. My lips are sealed,' Edwina told her firmly. 'I must say that this whole business sounds desperately complicated. But you're a big girl now, Sam. And, although I love you very much, I do realise that I've got to leave you to lead your own life. All the same,' she added with a sigh, 'Matt really *is* gorgeous. And I can quite see why you're prepared to give the relationship a second go. I expect I would, too, under the circumstances. Do you think...is there any chance you could both get serious about one another?'

Samantha shook her head. 'No. It's not that sort of relationship. So, I don't want any heavy hints about wedding bells—because neither of us is interested in any long-term commitment,' she told her sister firmly. 'Besides, having made one disastrous mistake, I'm sure as hell not going to rush into another!'

'Oh, Sam...' Edwina sighed and shook her head. 'You're *such* an idiot sometimes! I mean—just look at you. You're beautiful, sexy, highly successful at work, and earning pots of money. In fact, compared to so many other people, you've already achieved so much. So why keep reminding yourself about a mistake you made ages ago? It's time you put the whole incident behind you and got on with finding a man who *will* make you happy.'

'Thanks for the vote of confidence.' Samantha smiled mistily at her sister, deeply touched by the obvious love and affection embodied in her words of wisdom. 'All the same,' she added slowly, 'if I could make such a spectacular mess of things once... How on earth can anyone make sure that they *never* make the same mistake again?'

'They can't,' Edwina told her simply. 'However, if you listen to your heart, you'll *know* when you've found the person with whom you want to spend the rest of your days.

'Actually, that's the easy bit,' she added with a laugh as she opened the oven door to check how the roast chicken was coming along. 'It's making the relationship work—day in and day out, through good times and bad—which can sometimes be very hard work. You just have to hang in there. Always having faith and trust in one another is what counts in the end.'

'Mummy...?' Olivia, the eldest of her two daughters, suddenly burst into the kitchen. 'Mr Warner and Daddy are having a drink in the sitting room—and want to know whether you and Aunt Sam would like one, too. And can we *please* take Mr Warner out to see the ponies?' she continued in a rush. 'It's still not too dark, and...'

'Hold it!' her mother laughed. 'Yes, Sam and I would love a glass of wine. And no—you can't drag poor Mr Warner off to the stables at this late hour. Besides, it's time for you and Rosie to have a bath and go to bed. You can show him the ponies tomorrow morning. But, for goodness' sake, don't wake the poor man up too early. OK?'

'Which reminds me...' Edwina said as her young

daughter gave a heavy sigh and left the room. 'I hope that I've made the right sleeping arrangements?' She gazed at Samantha with a worried frown. 'I mean...I wasn't exactly sure, from what you said on the phone, whether you and Matt were...er...'

'Relax!' Samantha grinned, taking pity on her older sister. 'Yes, we are sleeping together. But, no, it doesn't matter about giving us separate rooms. For one thing, this is your house. And I know that you and David would always prefer your guests to respect the family atmosphere. And besides,' she added, 'I don't think it's ideal for either Olivia or Rosie to rush into my bedroom, first thing in the morning—as they have a habit of doing—to find someone else in bed with me.'

'I'm so glad you see it that way,' her sister murmured, clearly relieved to have her own judgement confirmed. 'I realise, modern-day life being what it is, Olivia probably knows more about the facts of life than I do!' Edwina gave a wry bark of laughter. 'But I already have *so* many questions to answer, I can well do without any more!'

'The joys of motherhood...?' Samantha grinned.

'You wait! You won't find it so funny—not when you've got your own children watching TV, and subsequently demanding to know exactly what HIV means, or expecting you to help them with their maths homework. Believe me, it's *exhausting*!'

'I'm not sure that I'm ever going to be into having children,' Samantha mused slowly. 'I wouldn't ever want to give up my career, and...'

'Rubbish!' Her sister laughed. 'I thought you were a feminist? The sort of woman who believes that you can have your cake and eat it too?' she added sardonically.

'Well...'

'Don't worry, Sam. You'll find, if and when you do get married and have children, that it is quite possible to keep on working, as so many of my friends seem to be able to do. It's just that you have to run twice as fast,'

she added. 'What a pity that you can only stay one night.
If only to view your dear sister running herself ragged,
trying to cope with merely two daughters and no job!'

Samantha grinned. 'We all know that you can manage
with one hand tied behind your back,' she teased. 'But
I'm sorry we have to go back so soon. Unfortunately,
Matt's only over here for a brief visit. He's having to fly
back to the States on Sunday. So, I'm afraid we'll have
to leave after Rosie's party tomorrow afternoon.'

'Well, at least you'll still be here when Georgie ar-
rives,' her sister said. 'I've had our younger sister on the
phone this morning. She's promised to arrive in time for
the party, but was getting worried that she might not have
the chance of meeting your "new squeeze"!'

'Oh, Lord!' Samantha groaned.

'Yes, well…I'll do my best to see that she doesn't
cause you too much embarrassment,' Edwina promised.
'She really doesn't mean to say or do the wrong thing.
It's just…'

'I know,' Samantha agreed heavily. 'It's just that
Georgie is quite incapable of keeping her mouth shut!
However, there's no point in worrying about something
clearly beyond anyone's control.' She shrugged. 'I think
I'll just go upstairs and freshen up before dinner. OK?'

Making her way up the stairs and along the landing of
the old house, Samantha was startled, on entering her
small room, to find Matt lying stretched out on her bed.

'I thought you were having a drink with David?'

'Yes, I was enjoying his company. In fact, your
brother-in-law is an exceptionally nice and extremely intelligent man,' he drawled, swinging his long legs off the
bed. 'But I thought I'd try and have a word with you,
while everyone is still downstairs.'

'Is there a problem?' she asked anxiously, wondering
what on earth could have gone wrong, so soon after their
arrival.

'A problem? Good heavens, no!' he drawled with

heavy sarcasm, coming over to put his arms about her slim figure.

'I'm absolutely *delighted* to find my bedroom is down a long corridor, simply miles away from your room. I'm utterly *entranced* to discover that every single floorboard of the said corridor squeaks like a banshee. And I'm simply *over the moon*,' he added through gritted teeth, 'that I've got about as much chance of making love to you tonight as I have of suddenly discovering the secret of the universe!'

'Oh, Matt,' she giggled.

'Don't you *dare* laugh at me, you wretch!' he growled, pulling her tightly up against his hard, strong body. 'It's been six weeks since I held you in my arms. Believe me, you're looking at a desperate man!'

'Well…that's nice!' She smiled at him as she wound her arms up about his neck. 'Unfortunately, we shall both just have to exercise some control, won't we?' she teased.

'Congratulations on your self-discipline, Sam!' he breathed thickly, raising a hand to pluck away the combs holding up the hair on top of her head, and allowing the long, heavy mass to tumble down about her shoulders.

'Unfortunately, I'm not *nearly* so strong-minded,' he added huskily, burying his fingers in the pale, silky strands and holding her head firmly beneath him as his mouth came down to take possession of hers, parting her lips and devouring the sweetness within her mouth with ruthless determination.

She moaned helplessly as he pushed her gently backwards, until she found herself pinned up against the oak door of her bedroom by his muscular body, and in no doubt of his barely suppressed, rampant arousal.

His lips gradually softened, slowly moving over hers with a languorous sensuality, which provoked an instantaneous, passionate response in her trembling body. Swept by a riptide of fierce passion and excitement, pulsating through each and every fibre of her being, Samantha could only cling helplessly to his broad shoulders as she responded feverishly to his kiss.

Slowly raising his head, Matt stared down at the soft, trembling temptation of her lips, and the long eyelashes, fluttering helplessly as she gazed blindly up at him, totally in the grip of a torrent of passion and desire.

'*Sweetheart...!*' he groaned softly, burying his face in her hair, savouring its fresh, clean scent for a moment before gradually pulling himself together.

'I'm sorry, darling—I got carried away for a moment or two,' he murmured huskily. 'My only excuse is that six weeks has proved to be a much longer time than even I had anticipated,' he added ruefully.

'That...that makes two of us,' she murmured, desperately trying to drag herself back from the wilder shores of lust to some form of normal, everyday existence. 'Why don't you go on downstairs, while I just fix my hair? I'll follow you in a minute.'

He shook his dark head. 'Oh, no. We'll go downstairs together,' he told her firmly. 'I'm not even going to try and pretend that we haven't been having a highly romantic encounter up here. Besides,' he added with a low, ironic laugh, 'I don't think either of us is particularly good at hiding our emotions.'

Samantha was well aware of her sister casting speculative glances at both Matt and herself during dinner. But her husband, David, was a far too prosaic, down-to-earth character to be interested in delving into any speculation about his guests. So, Edwina had no choice but to follow his lead.

Although Samantha had been dreading the arrival of her younger sister, in the event it proved not to be the awful ordeal she'd feared.

Having hitched a lift from one of her many boyfriends, Georgie airily told the rather vacuous-looking youth that she would expect both him and his smart sports car to be outside the farmhouse in four hours' time.

'Well—off you go, Hugo,' she added impatiently, dismissing the devoted swain, and clearly forgetting all about him by the time she walked in the front door.

'Oh-ho! So, *you're* the man of the moment who's currently keeping my sister's bed warm?' she queried, giving Matt a broad smile, while her two older sisters cringed in embarrassment.

But Matt, who'd swiftly and accurately summed up the situation, merely gave Samantha's beautiful young sister a cool smile.

'Yes, you're quite right. She's just using me for sex,' he drawled smoothly. 'However, I'm sure that we're all far more interested in hearing about *you*. Exactly how many men of the moment are you currently using as a hot-water bottle?'

There was a stunned silence following his words, with Georgie staring at him blank-faced for a moment, before she threw back her head and gave a peal of laughter.

'Hey—you're all right! Not at all the sort of stuffed shirt I was expecting to meet.' She grinned.

'No, I only wear my shirts stuffed during the week,' he assured her blandly. 'At weekends, I like to relax and attend birthday parties. Shall I take you to join the *other* children?' he added, the heavy irony clearly going straight over her head as Georgie beamed happily up at him; then he led the way out through the house to the garden, where the party was in full swing.

Edwina and Samantha stared at one another, breathing a collective sigh of both relief and amazement.

'I'll tell you what, Sam,' her sister finally said in awe-struck tones. 'If you've got any sense in that beautiful head of yours, I reckon you'd be a fool not to drag that man up to the altar—as soon as possible! For what it's worth, he's certainly got *my* vote of approval.'

As it turned out, Georgie was so clearly entranced to

actually meet someone prepared to be, if necessary, even blunter than herself that the rest of the afternoon passed by without any upsets. In fact, as Matt confessed on their drive back to London, he'd thoroughly enjoyed meeting *all* Samantha's family.

'Even Georgie?' She grinned.

'To be honest, it was fun teasing your younger sister,' he said. 'There really isn't an ounce of malice in the girl. And, let's face it, she merely puts into words what everyone else is thinking—but far too polite or inhibited to say out loud. Maybe we should all stop being so well-behaved, and take a leaf out of Georgie's book,' he mused reflectively.

'Life certainly wouldn't be dull!' Samantha laughed. 'Now, we're coming into Central London. Which hotel are you staying at?'

'*Sa-man-tha…!*' he groaned. 'I've never heard anything so stupid. Have you entirely lost your mind? Why on earth would I want to stay in a hotel?'

'Well, I hadn't really thought much about it,' she muttered, her cheeks flushing. 'I mean…I just assumed, now that you're a captain of industry and all that sort of thing…'

'That's very flattering, of course. But, if it's all the same to you, I'd much rather spend the night in your apartment. Or is there any reason why I wouldn't be welcome?'

She didn't immediately answer, her attention being claimed for some time by the need to drive carefully through the heavy Saturday evening traffic.

'I may have assumed that you'd have been booked into the Ritz or the Dorchester, for business reasons,' she told him finally as they entered the underground car park beneath her apartment. 'But for you to think that you wouldn't be welcome to stay with me really *is* stupid.'

'*Touché!*' Matt laughed. She parked the car, and they began walking over to the elevator. 'Right…' he added as she punched the button for her floor. 'I'm giving you precisely ten seconds from the moment we enter your apartment. And if you are *still* wearing any clothes after that time I refuse to be responsible for my actions!'

'Oh, really?' she laughed. 'And what about you?'

'Oh, don't worry,' he murmured, leaning across to give her a quick kiss. 'I shall be undressed and in your bed, stop-watch in hand, long before you've even begun taking the combs out of your hair. And *that's* a promise!' he vowed, sealing his words with another kiss.

It was still pitch-dark when Samantha surfaced from a deep sleep. Turning her head, she saw from the luminous dial of her bedside clock that it was just after three in the morning.

She slowly stretched her body, which still felt heavy and languorous after a night of passion. As always, their lovemaking had been so breathtaking and indescribably perfect that if Samantha hadn't been such a down-to-earth person she might have thought that she'd been in paradise.

Heaven can wait, she told herself, smiling in the darkness. Certainly for a few more years. She was only concerned with the present—the vital personality and the flesh and blood of the man who'd raised her to such heights of unimaginable pleasure.

Putting out a hand to touch his sleeping form, she was surprised to find that Matt was not in the bed beside her. He must have just gone to the bathroom, she thought idly, settling the pillows more comfortably behind her head and lapsing back into a delicious recollection of all they had done and said to one another that night.

However, as she once again opened her eyes and saw that it was nearly half an hour since she'd discovered his absence, Samantha frowned, before suddenly realising that he might not be well. Or perhaps the *confit* of duck, which she'd hastily thrown together for a late supper, might not have agreed with him.

Quickly switching on her bedside light, she got out of bed. Slipping on a light robe to cover her nakedness, she padded silently out of the bedroom and across the large main sitting room, towards where she could see a dim glow of light, from the kitchen.

Unaware of her presence as she stood in the kitchen doorway, her bare feet having made no sound as she'd moved over the oak wooden flooring, Matt had his back towards her as he leant against the kitchen cupboard on the other side of the room. Sleepily blinking, she was just opening her mouth to enquire whether he was feeling all right, when she saw he was speaking rapidly into a small mobile phone.

'Well, you're just going to have to firm up some support from the shareholders,' he was saying. Even from across the room she could hear the grim, tense note in his low voice, before a slight movement caught the peripheral edge of his vision and he turned to see Samantha standing in the doorway.

'I'll be in touch,' he muttered quickly, swiftly slamming the phone shut before walking towards her. 'Did I wake you up, darling?'

'No...' She raised a hand to rub the sleep out of her eyes. 'No...but I was just wondering where you'd got to. I thought you might be ill, or something.'

Matt gave a low laugh. 'Far from feeling ill, I've never felt better in my whole life!' he murmured huskily, putting his arm around her waist and leading her slowly back through the large, empty sitting room towards her bedroom.

'But...but what were you doing?' she asked, finding it difficult to concentrate on anything other than the featherlight touch of his fingers on her skin as he slowly removed her light wrap. 'Who...who were you talking to?'

'Nobody important,' he muttered, his strong arms tightening possessively as he gently drew her up against him. 'My lovely, exciting Samantha,' he breathed, clearly savouring each moment as his hands moved leisurely over her warm, pliant flesh towards the aroused peaks of her breasts, swollen and aching in anticipation of his touch. 'How gloriously soft your skin is—smooth and silky as velvet.'

And then the feel of his own warm body against hers was so exquisite, and with her overwhelming compulsion to respond to his urgent touch, her whole being vibrating in response to his sensual arousal, Samantha completely lost any interest in the phone conversation which Matt had been having in the kitchen, surrendering eagerly to the extraordinary, heart-stopping pleasure of his warm lips moving slowly and seductively over her flesh.

It was only much later, lying securely clasped within his arms as they both slowly slipped into a deep sleep, that Samantha recalled Matt's use of the mobile phone. But it had nothing to do with her. So why should she care whom he was calling at that hour of the night?

CHAPTER FIVE

SAYING goodbye to your lover, amidst the crowds and noise of Heathrow airport on a Sunday afternoon, was the absolute pits! Samantha told herself grimly on her return to the empty apartment.

Tossing her car keys down on to the hall table and checking her answering machine on the slim chance that Matt had left a loving message before boarding his plane—which, of course, he hadn't—she wandered disconsolately through the large, silent space of her main sitting room.

Unfortunately, she was still feeling so strung up with nervous tension that the normally peaceful and quiet atmosphere was totally failing to soothe her troubled mind.

Maybe you're just not mistress material? Maybe you really aren't cut out for this 'hello and goodbye' sort of lifestyle? she said to herself glumly. Because there was no doubt that she was now feeling utterly miserable and deeply unhappy at the prospect of, once again, not seeing Matt for some time.

Come on! Pull yourself together, she told herself roughly—as she'd been forced to do so often since their first meeting in New York, nearly two months ago. She had to stop moaning away at herself like this. Not only was it a stupid waste of time, but for a woman of her age it was nothing less than totally pathetic.

Having given herself a good talking-to, Samantha trailed off into the kitchen to make herself a soothing cup of tea. And later, planting up some of the geraniums which she'd ordered to brighten up her rooftop terrace, she found herself able to take a more detached, sensible view of the situation.

If she felt tired and depressed, poor Matt was likely to be exhausted by the time his plane landed in New York. Quite frankly, how the poor guy managed on so little sleep she had absolutely no idea.

Waking up early this morning, Samantha had found that, once again, she was alone in her bed.

Seven o'clock in the morning…? Where on earth had he got to *this* time? she'd grumbled to herself, before slipping out of bed, putting on a dressing gown and wandering sleepily into the main room.

Well, she ought to have known that a workaholic would be working! she'd told herself, ruefully eyeing the sight of Matt sitting at her desk, mobile phone in one hand, a pen in the other.

'Hi, sweetheart,' he'd muttered, giving a brief wave of the hand before quickly resuming his phone conversation and concentrating on the work in front of him.

Wandering into the kitchen and switching on the coffee percolator, Samantha had found herself thinking that although Matt's tall frame and broad shoulders had been clothed in her own dark blue towelling dressing gown—which was clearly far too small—he'd still managed to look diabolically attractive.

However, by the time she'd had a long, leisurely bath, taken some time in rejecting a summer dress in favour of a slim-cut pair of white linen trousers and a pale blue linen shirt, she wasn't feeling quite so sanguine. In fact, after having read the Sunday newspapers from cover to cover, Samantha had found herself taking a far more jaundiced view of Matt's tall, broad-shouldered figure.

'Hello…? Is there anyone there…?' she called out, after glancing down at her watch and noting that it was almost lunchtime.

'Hmm…?'

'Hi! Remember me?' she ground out sarcastically, rolling her eyes up to the ceiling in exasperation as he turned to gaze at her in surprise. 'Come on, Matt—give us both a break,' she added with a helpless shrug. 'You can't be intending to work *all* day, surely?'

He sighed, putting down his pen and turning around in his chair to face her. 'I'm sorry, darling. I know it's a real drag—but I really *must* sort out this work before a directors' meeting first thing on Monday morning. The fact is…' He hesitated for a moment, before giving a heavy sigh. 'The fact is that I really shouldn't be here at all. I've got umpteen business problems to cope with, and taking off this weekend to meet up with you—which I very much wanted to do—has meant that I'm now scrambling to get my work done on time.'

'I do understand,' she muttered. 'But…'

He rose from the chair and came over to sit down beside her on the sofa. 'But…this sort of brief meeting isn't very satisfactory, for either of us,' he agreed softly, slipping his arm around her shoulders and holding her tightly against his hard chest. 'I'm sorry, sweetheart…' he murmured, burying his face in fragrant clouds of her pale blonde hair.

'Well…I'm sorry, too, Matt. I shouldn't have been such a grouch. It's obvious that you're heavily involved with business at the moment.'

He gave a short bark of sardonic laughter. 'That, as it happens, is putting it mildly! And it's not going to get any easier, for the foreseeable future,' he added grimly, before firmly grasping her shoulders and holding her away from him as he gazed intently down into her blue eyes.

'It's obviously important that we're always utterly frank with one another,' he told her. 'So, I'm going to have to admit that, however much I regret it—and despite anything I can personally do about the situation—it's very likely that I'm not going to be in a position to see much of you during the coming months.'

'Well, I guess that's the way the cookie crumbles,' she said, doing her best to hide her deep disappointment and feelings of unhappiness at what he'd just said. 'Business comes first—right?' she added lightly.

'Yes,' he nodded. 'In this case, yes, I'm afraid it does.'

And that, Samantha now told herself as she took a step backwards, admiring the sight of her newly planted pots of geraniums—that had been virtually his last word on the subject. Because, after quickly showering and once again putting on his formal business suit, then having a quick lunch, it had been time for her to drive him to the airport.

The journey had not been a comfortable one, certainly as far as she was concerned. Seemingly sunk into some deep, internal reverie, Matt had remained virtually silent throughout the drive. And he'd seemed to mentally withdraw from her, as well, which had the strange effect of making her hesitant and nervous about disturbing the inner concentration of a man who—now light years away from the warm, tender lover of last night—had become a disturbingly withdrawn, coldly austere, forbidding personality, who clearly would not welcome any idle conversation.

Their farewell had been brief and hurried. Indeed, in direct contrast to his ebullient embrace on his arrival only two days ago, Matt had merely given her a quick peck on the cheek, muttered, 'I'll be in touch, sweetheart,' and swiftly disappeared in the direction of the airport's first-class lounge.

The plain fact was, Samantha told herself now as she tidied up her terrace, putting away her garden tools before sinking down onto one of the pretty white iron chairs around a large circular table, she really wasn't at all sure that she would ever hear from him again.

It was, of course, only a very strong gut feeling. And not one that she could necessarily fully justify. But Matt was proving to be very much of an enigma. And, while she had no doubt at all about the strength of feeling produced by their strong sexual attraction to one another, she still had no idea of what was *really* going through his mind.

Matt had declared, at the beginning of their relationship almost two months ago, that he wanted a love affair—while, at the same time, making it quite clear that it would not include any emotional ties. While she, for her part, had agreed that she could handle it. And so she had. The trouble was...well, she was no longer *quite* so certain that she was fully in command of her emotions.

If this was just a passing fling—a brief love affair between two consenting adults—it really shouldn't matter if he *had* suddenly decided to call it a day. And she ought not to be too upset if she didn't hear from him again. But unfortunately it was now highly disturbing to discover that the thought of never seeing Matt again was causing her to feel utterly bereft and deeply unhappy.

So, something had clearly gone wrong with the original scenario—right? But exactly *why* she was feeling like this, and how to cope with it, seemed entirely beyond her at the moment.

With the usual blind luck and good fortune attracted by fools and idiots, it seemed that Henry Graham was, after all, going to win the office sweepstake, and thus scoop the pool.

So much was evident on her arrival at work the next day, when Samantha was taken totally by surprise to find herself being called up into the chairman's office—and offered the job previously held by her boss, Paul Unwin.

She was thrilled. Yes, of course she was. Who wouldn't be both excited and elated to have achieved this promotion, and at such a young age? A point which the chairman himself made very clear.

'I'm a great believer in giving youngsters their heads,' he said as she sat perched on the edge of a chair, in front of his desk. 'And I'm sure that you will justify our belief in your ability. In fact,' he added with what appeared to be a distinct twinkle in his eye, 'I have to say that your expertise in managing to cope with that young layabout, Henry Graham, has not gone unnoticed.'

Well, well! Maybe having Dopey Henry foisted onto her hadn't been such a bad career move after all, Samantha told herself with a slight, inward grin.

However, as the chairman went on to outline her new responsibilities, she found her attention slipping away, as it seemed to be doing so often these days.

Mentally making a note of the people whom she must ring and tell the good news, Samantha quickly added her parents to the list. Her father and mother might be difficult to contact—especially since they were currently sailing around the Caribbean islands—but nevertheless they were going to be thrilled to hear about her promotion.

However, above and beyond anything else, she desperately wanted to be able to tell Matt about her new job. Although why it should be quite so important that she tell *him* she wasn't quite sure...

'Well, Miss Thomas, you seem to be taking this all in a very sanguine, laid-back manner,' the chairman was saying, regarding the girl in front of his desk with some amusement.

Clearly possessing considerable talents, besides also being disturbingly good-looking, she appeared to be remarkably unperturbed by the weight of her new responsibilities. But that was youth, he told himself with an inward, heavy sigh. And, although he was only in his forties, maybe it was time he thought about handing over to the next generation?

Idly wondering how the cool, calm and collected Miss Thomas might respond if he 'rattled her cage' just a little, he took the opportunity to point out that her new job wasn't going to be all plain sailing.

'You do realise, I take it, that there may well be trouble in store?'

'Trouble?' Her blue eyes sharpened as she clearly threw off her abstraction, immediately concentrating her full attention on what he was saying. 'Exactly what sort of trouble are you talking about?'

'There is a possibility—although I can't really say any more at this stage—that we may be involved in a very acrimonious take-over battle.'

'If we're involved, it must mean that we have large holdings in each firm. So, which companies are we talking about?' she asked quickly.

Satisfied that he had her full attention and that she was, as he had hoped, as sharp as a needle, the chairman leaned back in his chair.

'I can't give you that information at the moment. I'm still waiting for final confirmation from my sources,' he added with a shrug. 'However, I'll keep you informed as soon as I hear anything definite.'

'Congratulations, and all that jazz!' Henry exclaimed, clearly pleased as punch as he strolled into her office, following Samantha's interview with the chairman.

'*You* may only just have heard the news,' he added with a grin. 'However, I can tell you this place is already buzzing about your promotion.'

'I might have known that the office scuttlebutt would be better informed than I was.' Samantha grinned, unable to hide the pleasure and excitement she felt over her new appointment.

'I must say, everyone seems very pleased for you—although there are some people who don't look *too* happy about the situation, of course!'

She nodded. It was easy to understand why her colleagues might resent someone younger than themselves being promoted over their heads and given so much responsibility. And it wasn't only her promotion which might have upset them. Even she had been absolutely astounded to learn, from a casual remark of the chairman's, that she was now likely to be earning well over half a million pounds a year.

In fact, if she were living and working in America, she'd probably be entitled to refer to herself as a one hundred per cent, genuine millionaire!

Quickly suppressing a slightly hysterical giggle at the thought of her sudden elevation into the ranks of the very rich, Samantha was soon brought down to earth by the necessity to deal with practical matters. Such as moving into her new and much larger office.

It was only when Samantha was seated in the large, comfortable chair, behind an equally large, leather-covered mahogany desk, that the full reality of her position finally hit home.

Almost unbelievably, she really *was* the new boss on this floor of the large organisation! And as such, of course, her shoulders were going to have to bear a heavy weight of responsibility.

But all that lay in the future. Just for the moment, she felt entitled to give herself a small, private pat on the back. Because—glory be!—at what was a relatively young age she'd finally *made it*!

'Well…this is more like it!' Henry exclaimed, standing in the doorway and regarding her new, far more spacious office with considerable satisfaction, before handing her a hot cup of strong coffee.

'Bless you, Henry! This is just what I needed, after hauling all my stuff into this office.'

He laughed. 'I knew it was only a matter of time before you began to appreciate my sterling qualities,' he agreed blandly, the smile quickly draining from his lips as the girl behind the desk gave a sudden gasp.

'For heaven's sake, Sam. Are you all right?' he asked, frowning with concern as she swiftly clasped her hands together over her stomach, leaning forward in her chair, her face growing pale and strained.

She gave a silent nod of her head, waiting for the violently nauseous feeling in her stomach to subside, as it always did, before explaining that she wasn't feeling too good just at the moment.

'I'll be all right in a minute,' she muttered. 'Just forget it—OK?'

'No, I won't forget it,' he retorted tersely. 'Have you seen a doctor? For heaven's sake, Sam—it could be something quite serious, like appendicitis.'

'No, I'm quite sure it's nothing like that,' she said firmly. 'However, as it happens, I *have* made up my mind to see a doctor. Quite frankly, I think that it's probably just a virus of some sort. Nothing to worry about.'

'OK…just as long as you *do* go and see a doctor.' Henry viewed her pale face with considerable concern. 'I know you, Sam. I reckon you'll come up with at least a hundred reasons for putting it off.'

'Don't nag!' she snapped.

But she ought to have known that Henry was quite unsnubbable. Maintaining that he saw it as one of his duties to keep her as healthy and wealthy as possible, he refused to drop the subject. So, purely in self-defence, she found herself being forced to make the phone call to a Harley Street medical centre, highly recommended by Henry.

Waiting impatiently as the doctor's receptionist hummed and hawed her way through the appointments book, Samantha found herself being distracted by her assistant, who was insisting on trying to tell her about some company take-over.

'Yes, as soon as possible,' she told the receptionist, before placing a hand quickly over the phone and turning to her assistant. 'Put a sock in it, Henry! I can't do two things at once,' she muttered, before resuming her conversation with the doctor's receptionist. 'Yes, yes, that'll be fine. I can make five o'clock this afternoon. No problem.'

Putting down the phone, and making a quick note in her diary, she turned back to Henry. 'OK... Now, what is it you've been jabbering on about?'

'I was merely wondering if you've heard anything about Broadwood Securities?'

'Broadwood...?' she murmured, becoming very still for a moment, before carelessly fiddling with a pencil on her desk. Henry might well be a fool, as far as financial investment was concerned, but there was no doubt that he was extremely street-smart. And she had no intention of giving him any indication that Matt's company had any significance for her whatsoever.

'What have you heard?' she continued, as though the whole subject had no interest for her. 'Anything interesting?'

Henry shrugged his shoulders. 'Well, I can't even say that it's got the status of a rumour,' he admitted. 'However, when I was at my parents' home, over the weekend, I did overhear my old dad on the phone to one of his cronies. I could have got it all wrong, of course. But it did sound as though he was referring to some take-over battle between Broadwood Securities and another outfit— although I didn't catch their name.'

Samantha relaxed slightly. Trust Henry to get the wrong end of the stick, as usual, she told herself wryly.

'As far as I'm aware, there's absolutely *no* possibility of Broadwood being taken over,' she told him firmly. 'For one thing, it's such a large firm that any serious, aggressive attack by another company would be common knowledge by now. Still,' she added with a slight shrug, 'it's no bad thing to keep your ear to the ground. Unfortunately, Henry, I'm afraid that this is one time when you've picked the wrong horse!'

Grinning privately to herself as he rose to his feet and ambled out of the office, Samantha wished that all such wild rumours were as easy to evaluate as the one which Henry thought he'd picked up. Because, of course, if there *had* been any question of Broadwood being under threat, Matt would have told her straight away, wouldn't he?

Matthew Warner's intelligence operation appeared to be a lot better than her own, Samantha decided a few days later, when she received an enormous bouquet of deep crimson roses, together with a message from Matt, congratulating her on her new job.

How on earth did he manage to find out so soon? she asked herself, before quickly realising that it was a stupid question. It was as much his job as hers to keep an ear to the financial ground. In fact, with a whole horde of personal assistants at his command, he was likely to be far more ahead of the game than she was. As confirmed by his phone call a few days later.

'Well done, Miss Thomas! We always knew you had it in you,' he said, his amusement clearly audible down the line. 'How does it feel to be boss of your new department?'

'A bit scary,' she confessed, suddenly feeling extraordinarily happy and cheerful at hearing his voice once again. 'How's New York?'

He gave a loud, theatrical groan. 'Busy, busy, *busy*! Otherwise we'd have an opportunity to celebrate your new appointment in style,' he told her. 'Unfortunately, it doesn't look as though I'm going to be able to get over to London for some time. Even if I do manage a flying visit, it's going to be almost impossible to find time to see you.'

'Oh…right,' she muttered, suddenly realising that she might have been right about him not wanting to see her again, after all.

But Matt, who'd always been extremely perceptive as far as she was concerned, had immediately picked up the tight note of constraint in her voice.

'There's nothing I can do about it, Sam,' he told her firmly. 'There's a whole lot of things we need to talk about. But not now—and definitely not on the telephone.'

'OK…I understand. That's fine by me,' she told him, in her best imitation of her sister Georgie's airy, breezy tone of voice, which the younger girl had frequently used when dealing with her unfortunate boyfriends. If Matt thought he was giving *her* the runaround, Samantha was damned if she'd let him know how much it hurt.

'You don't understand…'

'Oh, really? And just *what* don't I understand?' she retorted swiftly in her normal voice. 'It seems pretty straightforward to me. One, you're very busy. Two, you can't see me for some time, up to and including the foreseeable future. And three, even if you *do* happen to find yourself in London, you're going to be far too busy for us to meet. Quite honestly, Matt,' she added with a shrill, high-pitched laugh, 'I'd say that you've made yourself *crystal*-clear!'

'Oh, for God's sake!' He swore down the line. 'Things are a lot more complicated than you seem to realise. Which is why I can't go into everything right now, on the phone. We need to have a long talk together, and—'

'OK…fine…I've got the message,' she interrupted him curtly. 'So, give me a call when you *can* find a small window in your diary. Now, I'm sorry, but I'll have to go. I've got another call on the line,' she added quickly, not giving him the opportunity to get a word in edgeways as she swiftly put down the phone.

'Damn, damn and double damn!' she muttered grimly under her breath, leaning back in her chair and staring blindly up at the ceiling.

Unfortunately, it was obvious that she hadn't handled that phone call at all well. In fact, why she should have gone so off the deep end, when she knew all about deadlines and pressure of work, she had no idea.

Maybe the truth was that this whole business of a long-distance love affair was getting her down. Despite all their best efforts, it was obvious that they were hardly going to be able to see much of each other, if at all. Besides, she was coming to see that any attempt to merge or accommodate their different lifestyles—however possible it might have seemed originally—simply wasn't going to work in practice. And, despite the fact that she and Matt might have a very strong sexual attraction for one another, what was the point of trying to maintain an ongoing relationship when they were going to see virtually nothing of one another?

These questions remained unanswered, continuing to trouble her during the rest of the week as she found herself having to cope with her new, frantically busy life.

Having somehow found the time to keep her appointment with the doctor, chair various group meetings of market analysts and investment managers, as well as familiarise herself with her new workload, when Henry told her that the chairman would like to see her that afternoon, one day, Samantha couldn't help feeling that this was one meeting she could have done without.

However, on entering the chairman's palatial office, she took the opportunity to thank him, once again, for placing his trust in her, and promised to do all she could to make a success of her new appointment.

'Yes...yes, we're all quite confident that you can cope with the job,' he told her with a smile, before waving to a chair in front of his desk.

'However,' he continued as she sat down in front of him, 'as I hinted, the other day, I'm afraid that you're now likely to find yourself facing an immediate baptism of fire.'

'I don't think that I quite understand...?' Samantha murmured.

Despite not wishing to look a fool—especially when she'd only just been appointed to the job—there was clearly no point in pretending that she knew what he was talking about. Because, quite frankly, she hadn't a clue.

The chairman hesitated for a moment. 'As you know, when a successful, medium-sized company decides to make an aggressive take-over bid for a much larger business, there are usually plenty of rumours flying about the City well before any action is taken.'

She nodded. A great deal of her time was spent listening to and evaluating rumours, as well as stray bits of news and gossip about forthcoming take-over battles.

'Unfortunately, I've now had confirmation, from a reliable source that there's a major confrontation looming. And it's one which is likely to involve this firm.'

'Oh…er…right,' Samantha responded, doing her best to look as if she was at least alert and on the ball. Although she couldn't for the life of her think of any recent titbit of news, rumour or even frankly scurrilous gossip which was likely to fit in with what her chairman was saying.

'As I understand it,' he continued, 'both the parties concerned, for quite separate reasons, were anxious to keep the news under wraps for as long as possible. And they would appear to have been successful. In fact, it's only now—with the news about to break—that there's been the first sniff of what's been going on in the background.'

Samantha frowned. 'Which two companies are we talking about?'

The chairman consulted some notes on the desk in front of him. 'It seems that the English and French consortium, Kendal-Laval Limited, is intending to break into the US market. Which is why they have decided to make a take-over bid for a much larger, American company—Broadwood Securities, Inc.'

'What…?'

'Yes,' the chairman nodded, mistaking her horrified exclamation for one of mere surprise. 'I, too, was taken aback by the news. However…'

But Samantha couldn't seem to absorb what else the chairman was saying, her whole mind being filled with one large question mark after another.

Because, of course, Broadwood Securities was Matt's company. Which meant…which meant that he *must* have known, for at least the past month, that his corporation was under threat, and in deadly danger of a take-over.

So—*why* on earth hadn't he told her? *Why* had he obviously felt unable to confide in her about the forthcoming battle? They were lovers—right? What possible reason could he have for deciding to remain totally silent about his problems…?

CHAPTER SIX

FEELING totally shocked and stunned by what she'd just heard, Samantha left the chairman's office in a daze.

Taking the elevator down to her own floor, she walked slowly through the deserted corridor leading to her office. It was by now the end of a long working day, and all her colleagues had obviously gone home, leaving only the silent army of security staff and office cleaners within the large building.

With a heavy sigh, Samantha sank down into the chair behind her desk, leaning back and staring up at the ceiling as she tried to get to grips with the situation that she now faced.

'You may well come to feel that we have handed you a poisoned chalice,' the chairman had told her earlier, his words accompanied by a thin-lipped, sardonic smile. And he'd been quite right. Although, of course, he had no idea of the extra, additional problems which she now faced.

In essence, it all boiled down to two vitally important questions: Did she have a conflict of interest in this case? And, if so, what the heck was she going to do about it?

The facts of the situation were very clear indeed.

Matthew Warner, chief executive of Broadwood Securities, was now facing an attempt by another, if smaller firm to take over, buy up and possibly dismantle his large company. And it looked as if the ensuing battle might prove to be very nasty, indeed.

Her chairman had not minced his words. 'It is likely to be a highly acrimonious, no-holds-barred fight,' he'd warned. 'It's been clear for some time that Broadwood had over-extended itself, and thus become vulnerable to just such a take-over. As I'm sure you're well aware.'

'Well…er…I don't have all the facts…'

'However, I understand that their newly appointed chief executive, Matthew Warner, has been ruthlessly sorting out the sheep from the goats, with the next half-yearly accounts likely to show a distinct improvement. Although even achieving that minor miracle may prove to be too little and too late to save his company.'

'What…er…what's the position of the two companies at the moment?' Samantha had asked through stiff lips, feeling distinctly sick as she struggled to master the seething ferment of fear and panic racing through her mind and body.

'My sources tell me that Kendal-Laval were determined to get their financial backers tightly sewn up before the news became public. In which they seem to have been successful,' the chairman had told her. 'As for Mr Warner—having obviously realised that an outside agency was buying up large blocks of his company's shares—I'm told, on good authority, that he's been working flat out to shore up his defences, get his Swiss bankers on side, and is now, I hear, digging in for a long, hard fight.'

'So, the battle lines have already been drawn up?'

'Oh, yes—I'm afraid so, my dear,' her boss had agreed with a rueful smile. 'So, we'll just have to wait and see which company will triumph in the end.'

Except, of course, that wasn't *strictly* true. Because, as her chairman had so accurately pointed out, it was a battle in which Minerva Utilities Management had not only a strong vested interest but they also held the balance of power. In other words the ultimate, casting vote.

He had also been very specific and down-to-earth about the problems she faced.

'Our firm, through its various pension fund investments, has a large holding in each of these two companies—who are about to go to war with each other,' he'd said. 'Sufficiently large, in fact, to swing the result one way or the other. So, it will be *our* decision—after carefully deciding which company offers the best investment for our clients—which will be absolutely crucial to the outcome of this take-over battle.'

'A real bed of thorns!' she'd muttered to herself, a point which had been immediately picked up by her chairman.

'Precisely!' He'd given a bark of dry, sardonic laughter. 'Especially as there's no doubt that it *will* be a very nasty, drag-out fight—with the press watching and commenting on every move. Incidentally,' he'd added, 'I've been tipped off that there is likely to be a long article about the take-over in the city paper. So, you must be very careful. No careless talk. And make sure that you avoid all journalists like the plague!'

Newspaper reporters were the *very least* of her problems, Samantha now told herself, almost groaning out loud as she leaned her elbows on the desk and buried her face in her hands, desperately trying to sort out the various arguments running frantically back and forth through her mind.

Talk about a really enormous can of worms!

What on earth was she going to do? Because there were some very worrying ethical and moral questions which she had to answer. Such as: what about her involvement with Matt?

It was maybe lucky that she'd told Henry to say she was out, if any calls came through from a Mr Warner. Because *if* she'd been taking his calls, and was also in the throes of an ongoing, passionate love affair with Matt, there was *no way* she could have taken on this job. Like Caesar's wife, she must be above suspicion.

Because, even if Samantha believed herself perfectly capable of taking an impartial decision between the two companies, no one else was going to see it that way!

All of which meant that she'd probably have to go to her chairman first thing tomorrow morning. And, after facing the horrendous embarrassment of explaining exactly *why* she had to declare a conflict of interest, request that she be taken off the case.

'*Oh, Lord!*' she groaned out loud, her shoulders sagging as she realised that her wonderfully enjoyable, fulfilling career was just about to hit the buffers—before quickly grinding to a shuddering halt.

'*Thank you for calling. Please leave a message, and I will get back to you as soon as possible.*'

Matt slammed down the phone in disgust. What the hell was that girl up to? And why wasn't she returning any of his telephone calls—not even when he left messages at her apartment?

Restless and angry, he rose from his chair to stretch his tired limbs, staring out of the large plate-glass window at the New York skyline.

So, OK...it was now a potentially delicate situation, businesswise. And maybe...maybe he *should* have told Samantha about the threat to his company from that two-bit European company. But surely she was far too sensible to hold that against him?

Working in the City herself, she must know the score. She knew how important it was to keep things under wraps. Besides, he *had* played fair. He *had* said that he might not be able to see her. Not that he'd really meant it, of course. How could he, when the thought of her lovely body was having such a disastrous effect on his ability to concentrate on the serious problems facing him?

His lips tightened with irritation—principally at himself for being such a fool. The trouble was, the damn girl had got under his skin. She was a very necessary part of his life now—and there seemed little he could do about the situation. Not at the moment, anyway, he told himself with a heavy sigh, trying to clear his mind of Samantha's beautiful face and slim, full-breasted figure as he sat down at his desk once more.

His gloomy thoughts were interrupted as one of his assistants knocked and entered his office.

'OK, sir. We've now got a complete breakdown of the figures,' the young man told him, clutching a thick file to his narrow chest. 'It looks certain that Minerva Utilities Management *will* have the casting vote.'

'It doesn't take a genius to see that,' Matt snapped irritably, not bothering to raise his dark head as he concentrated on signing some urgent letters. 'So, what else have you got for me?'

'Er…nothing, really. Except it really *would* be very helpful if we knew which way Minerva is going to swing their votes.'

'Indeed it would,' Matt murmured sarcastically. 'Unfortunately, not having a crystal ball to hand, we shall just have to concentrate on the figures, won't we?'

'Oh, I think we can do better than that, sir! I mean,' the young man added hurriedly as his boss raised his head, visibly wilting under the icy green glint in the older man's eyes, 'I think we really ought to try and make sure the result goes our way.'

'And just how do you propose to do that?' Matt queried, leaning back in his chair and regarding the young man with some interest.

'Well, sir—I reckon it might be a good idea to try and get on the right side of their new pension fund manager, Miss Samantha Thomas. You know, sort of sweet-talk the lady into…' His voice trailed away as his boss gave a harsh, sardonic bark of laughter.

'I can assure you,' Matt told him grimly, 'that Miss Thomas does not have a "right side" at the moment. I also happen to know that the idea of sweet-talking her into *anything*—up to and including answering the phone—is a pure waste of time!'

* * *

By the time she returned to her apartment that night, Samantha was beginning to get things sorted out in her mind, and feeling marginally less gloomy than she had earlier in the evening.

Unfortunately, her cautious optimism over the question of her job versus the state of her feelings for Matt lasted just as long as it took for her to check the calls on her answering machine.

'Hello, Sam.' Matt's strong, incisive tones flowed swiftly from the tape. *'You must be aware by now that I've been leaving messages for you at the office. So, why haven't I heard from you? We're both very busy, of course, but I really do need to contact you, fairly urgently. If you can't talk to me at work, give me a ring when you get home. OK?'*

There's no way I can talk to you, she told him silently as she sank wearily down on to the large sofa in the middle of the room. Not now. And most definitely not until she'd finally made up her mind about what she was going to do about this very, very difficult situation.

As far as she could see, it all came down to the question of just how involved she *was* with Matt Warner...

Trying to think clearly and logically as she later paced up and down her large sitting room, she continued to weigh up the pros and cons.

Yes...she and Matt had enjoyed a passionate affair in the past, many years ago. And yes...over the past eight weeks or so she'd spent two equally passionate weekends with the same man. However, since Matt—for some strange, completely mysterious reasons of his own—had quite deliberately kept her in the dark, Samantha could truthfully claim that she'd had no prior knowledge of the imminent take-over battle.

So, not only did she know nothing about what had been going on over the past two months—as far as Matt and his business was concerned—but she also had, at the present time, no in-depth information about the other company involved. Which meant that, as far as she was concerned, it really *was* a level playing field.

Leaving aside the deep anger bubbling away at the back of her head, regarding the fact that Matt had clearly not trusted her in any shape or form, she now realised that her basic instincts had been quite correct. It did very much look as though Matt had been swiftly backing out of her life ever since the last weekend they'd spent together—almost as quickly as he'd swept *into* her life two months ago in New York.

So, since he'd made it plain that he was *not* intending to see her in the immediate future, their brief love affair would appear to have been just that: short, sharp and now completely over.

Having finally arrived at the conclusion that she was morally and ethically in the clear—and that she could, with a good conscience, refute any charges of being too personally involved with one of the contenders, during the forthcoming take-over battle, Samantha had to admit to an enormous feeling of relief.

Besides, it might not come to a battle at all. The City of London was littered with companies who'd attempted to take over other firms—only to have their plans disrupted, one way or another. So, it made sense for her to sit tight. Do nothing. And wait and see which way the cookie crumbled.

However, having come to a reasoned, sensible decision about her present non-involvement with Matt, she still had the massive problem of having to deal with her own *personal* problems.

Unfortunately, they were far more tortuous and difficult to sort out than those to do with business...

What the hell did Matt think he was playing at? she raged silently, still feeling deeply troubled and as miserable as sin by the time she finally went to bed that night. If there was anyone whom you *should* be able to trust completely in this world, surely it ought to be your lover?

Although she and Matt had both been swept off their feet by a sudden, mutual passion for each other, they did have a past history of a warm and loving relationship. And, although she'd been totally devastated when that earlier affair had been so abruptly terminated, Samantha had always known, in her heart of hearts, that it had probably been inevitable. Indeed, with heavy pressure exerted by the university authorities—together with Matt's concern for her youth, inexperience and her future career—he'd probably had no choice but to behave as he did.

However, all those years ago, there had never been any underlying, hidden agenda. Absolutely the reverse. And, if she could now see that Matt had behaved cruelly, he had at least been ruthlessly honest and up-front about his reasons for doing so.

However, this time it was quite different. She wasn't a fool. She had gone into this renewal of their love affair with her eyes wide open. She'd always realised that the frantic, white heat of their mutual, overwhelming desire wasn't likely to last for ever. But she'd also believed that, when the frenzied urgency of their passion had faded—as it inevitably must sooner or later—they would at least remain good friends.

More fool you! she told herself roughly. Because, if she hadn't been entirely certain that she could handle their affair—fearing that she might become too emotionally involved with Matt—she *had* trusted him.

And why not? When they'd met up again in New York, he'd been brutally frank about his lack of long-term commitment, and had made it quite clear that he was only interested in a love affair. So, she'd known exactly where she stood. But at no point in their relationship had it ever occurred to her that he would quite deliberately *not* tell her about such a major development in his life as this forthcoming take-over battle.

Why...*why* hadn't he trusted her? Did he *seriously* believe that she was capable of doing something awful, like going to the newspapers and giving them details of his business affairs? Did he *really* think she was so shallow and untrustworthy?

Unfortunately, it now looked as if that was precisely what Matt had thought.

Well…to hell with him! she told herself defiantly. It was now clearly obvious that she'd never really known him at all. In fact, she ought to be deeply thankful that she wouldn't be seeing him any more.

However, despite her defiant thoughts, it was his sheer deception, together with a deep sense of betrayal, that now left her feeling so utterly devastated. If you haven't got trust in someone, you have *nothing*, was her last, despairing thought as she slipped into a deeply disturbed, restless sleep.

Burying herself in work was obviously one way of coping with personal problems, and over the next few days Samantha had the satisfaction of knowing that, while she might be feeling tired and weary, she'd also achieved a good deal.

She did have grave doubts about Henry's ability to keep his mouth shut about their firm's role in the takeover, of course. But there was little she could do, other than to warn him sternly of the dangers—hoping that he wouldn't get carried away and become indiscreet when out drinking with his friends.

On the plus side, however, all the members of her department were clearly excited by the challenge she'd set before them, with the research and analysis teams already hard at work preparing the necessary charts and data.

So far so good, Samantha told herself as she poured some hideously expensive oil into the bathtub after a hard day's work.

Lying back and relaxing in the hotly scented water, she could almost feel the strain and tensions of the day gradually seeping away from her weary mind and body.

Determinedly pushing any thought of Matt to the very back of her mind, she concentrated on making a mental list of all the things she had to do tomorrow.

It was a busy schedule, including not only an early morning visit to the doctor, to get the results of her tests—and hopefully some medicine to stop her feeling so tired and nauseous—but also a quick lunch with her sister.

Edwina, who was coming up to London to do some shopping, would undoubtedly have bought up most of Harrods by the time they met! Which, in fact, could prove to be a blessing. There should be no problem about keeping her sister's attention fully on her own purchases. Because, given half a chance, Edwina would almost certainly want to know all about the current state of her involvement with Matt.

Oh, no! She was definitely *not* going to think about him. Absolutely *not*! Samantha told herself fiercely, quickly getting out of the bath and roughly towelling herself dry. He was now history, right? So, the sooner she forgot all about him the better!

Unfortunately, that was something which was easier said than done. Slipping on a towelling dressing gown, she had just left the bathroom, and was walking through the main living room, when she was startled by the sharp, urgent ringing tone of the telephone.

As always—and especially at this late hour of the night—she allowed the call-screen facility to come into action, enabling her to check who was on the other end of the line, before deciding whether she wished to answer the phone.

'Sam…I'm still waiting for you to phone me.' She froze, completely unable to move as the sound of Matt's voice, harsh and impatient, echoed loudly around the main room of her apartment. *'I'm up to my eyeballs in work at the moment. Give me a ring at home, although I know the time difference makes things difficult. I don't know what the hell's going on. But we need to talk.'*

The faint click as he firmly replaced the phone without even, she noted grimly, a polite goodbye—let alone any endearment!—left her feeling shattered and trembling with nervous tension.

Even if she wished to, there was no way she could ring him back at his office. While the time difference he'd mentioned would mean her having to stay awake until three or four o'clock in the morning if she wanted to reach him at home. So, however much she might like to have a few, hard words with the rotten man, it was perhaps just as well that she wasn't going to have an opportunity to do so.

Unfortunately, she was so strung up following his phone call that it took her a long time before she fell into a restless sleep. And, once again, despite all her good intentions, there seemed nothing she could do to prevent Matt's lithe, tall, dark figure from striding arrogantly through her dreams. Which meant that she was already feeling washed out and exhausted as she left home to keep her first appointment of the day.

Samantha stared in open-mouthed shock and disbelief at the woman sitting on the other side of the desk.

'You must be joking!' she managed to croak at last, shaking her head as she desperately tried to make sense of this totally bizarre situation. 'I mean...I've never heard of anything so ridiculous.' She gave a high-pitched, incredulous laugh. 'Total claptrap!'

'The results plainly show...'

'Stuff and nonsense!' she exclaimed. 'I don't care *what* the so-called "results" may or may not show. Somebody has clearly made a bad mistake. You'll simply have to ask them to do the tests again. Because the whole idea is...well, it's just too absurd.'

And there were plenty of other, much ruder words she could have used to describe this farcical situation, Samantha told herself angrily. Quite apart from the fact that, once again, she'd overslept—what *was* wrong with her these days?—and should have been sitting at her desk in the office by now.

All of which meant that she *really* couldn't spare the time to listen to such rubbish. After all, she'd only made this appointment in the hope of clearing up a small problem—right? So, who needed this amount of grief and hassle?

She didn't want much, for heaven's sake. Merely a bottle of medicine. Nothing fancy. No bells and whistles. And certainly not anything requiring a Ph.D. in nuclear physics before being able to read the label. Just something to stop her feeling sick all the time. So, why wouldn't this stupid woman just get on with it, and write out a prescription?

The 'stupid woman' sitting behind the desk gave a heavy sigh. This situation was, of course, something she frequently had to face in her job. Which didn't make the present case any easier to deal with. However, as usual, she was simply going to have to talk matters through, slowly and steadily, until the girl in front of her managed to calm down—and listen to what she had to say.

'I'm afraid there is no possibility of error in this case, Miss Thomas,' she told Samantha. 'You're going to have to accept the fact that, as your doctor, I *do* know what I'm talking about.'

'But…but the whole idea is so ludicrous…' Samantha waved her hands distractedly in the air. 'I mean…'

'Nevertheless, you *are* pregnant,' the doctor continued in a firm but gentle voice. 'You *are* expecting a baby, which will be born in approximately seven months' time.' She leaned forward to consult a calendar on the desk in front of her. 'A January baby. That's nice.'

'*Nice…?*' Samantha gasped in horror, before lapsing into a stunned silence. This simply could *not* be happening to her. She…expecting a baby? Oh, no. There had to be some mistake. There just *had* to be!

The doctor gave another heavy sigh. 'Lets take it from the top, shall we?' she began, giving the girl a tired smile. 'You were engaged in a sexual relationship at some point in April?'

'Well…yes, I was,' Samantha admitted with a reluctant nod. 'But…'

'And were you taking adequate precautions?'

'Yes, of course,' she snapped.

'On each and every occasion?' the doctor queried. 'Please think very carefully, Miss Thomas,' she added patiently. 'Because there must have been at least *one* time when you were, perhaps, just a little careless…?'

'Absolutely not!' Samantha retorted swiftly, her cheeks flushing at the recollection of Matt's tender lovemaking, and the way in which he'd so carefully and adroitly ensured that she'd have no worries about the risk of conception.

Just about to open her mouth and firmly deny that she, or Matt, would have been so stupid as to ignore the principles of 'safe sex', Samantha suddenly realised that there had…maybe…been just the *one* occasion when they hadn't been so sensible.

Oh, my God! Could it be the result of the very first time they'd made love—both totally in the grip of a feverish, frantic explosion of overwhelming lust and passion—after dining at the Four Seasons, in New York? So overcome by their consuming need and desire for one another that they hadn't…there'd been no time to…

The doctor leaned back in her chair, watching the conflicting emotions flickering rapidly over the girl's pale features. 'So, there was at least one occasion when you didn't use any form of birth control?'

'Yes…' Samantha muttered, staring blindly down at the nervous, tensely clenched hands in her lap, before desperately trying to pull herself together. 'But…but it was only *once*. Surely it's not possible…?'

The doctor shook her grey head. 'A young, healthy

woman, under thirty years of age? Oh, yes, I'm afraid that it is only too possible,' she said wryly. 'Do I take it that you are not married?'

Samantha shook her head.

'And is that likely to prove a problem? Because if you need any help or counselling please feel free to contact me at any time.'

'Er…thank you,' Samantha muttered, still not really able to believe that she was pregnant.

However, by the time she left the doctor's consulting room, she'd finally realised that—totally and utterly incredible as it might seem—she really *was* going to have a child.

Leaving Harley Street, she wandered in a daze until she found herself standing outside a coffee shop in Marylebone High Street. Briefly managing to pull herself together, Samantha still took some moments, helplessly fumbling through her large handbag, before she located her mobile phone. And then, leaning weakly against a stone column in an empty doorway, she dialled her office. Mumbling some excuse about not feeling very well and that she was taking the day off, she entered the café and ordered a *very* strong cup of coffee.

You'd better make the most of this, she told herself grimly, recalling having read somewhere that caffeine was bad for expectant mothers—and only with great difficulty suppressing an urge to scream out loud in rage and frustration.

It wasn't that she *didn't* want to have a baby. It was just…well, she hadn't even got around to thinking about marriage, children, and all that sort of thing. That was a part of life which, up to now, she'd always thought of as being an experience which lay ahead of her. Something to look forward to, in the future. Not an urgent problem which needed to be dealt with here and now. Not when she'd just achieved the first great success of her career. And most definitely *not* when a brief love affair, with an old flame, had proved so disastrously short…and she never wanted to see the foul man ever again!

Oh, Lord! She'd been so preoccupied with her own problems that she'd completely forgotten all about Matt.

OK…OK…cool down! she warned herself urgently, suddenly feeling faint and dizzy.

Forcing herself to take a deep breath, and staring blankly down at the coffee cup in front of her, Samantha gradually calmed down as she tried to sort out the jumbled chaos in her brain.

You've got to relax…and stay very, very calm, she told herself desperately. In fact, you've absolutely *got* to think this through sensibly. Because how Matt was likely to react when he heard the news that she was expecting his baby was desperately important.

She'd always prided herself on being able to think rationally and logically about a problem. And this was definitely one time when she was going to need every ounce of clear-headed, practical and down-to-earth sense she could lay her hands on.

By the time she was on her second cup of coffee, Samantha had firmly rejected any thought of abortion. Whatever happened, she definitely *was* going to have her baby.

Right—that was one decision. Now for the one-million-dollar question: what was she going to do about Matt?

Even the thought of having to break the news to him was enough to make her feel faint and panic-stricken. Unfortunately, however much she dreaded the idea—because, of course, she had absolutely no idea how he would react to the news—there was no doubt in her mind that she must do so.

Matt might not welcome fatherhood. He could well feel, as she did, utter consternation and dismay that one brief moment of careless rapture could produce such a dramatic result. But she had no alternative. She must tell him. Because, quite simply, he had a moral right to know that, in the fullness of time, she would be giving birth to his baby.

'Sorry I'm late,' Samantha called out as she quickly threaded her way through the tables of the restaurant to where her sister, Edwina, was sitting. 'The...er...the traffic was awful, as usual.'

'I don't know how you can bear to live in London,' Edwina said as her younger sister gave her a quick peck on the cheek, before sitting down at the table beside her. 'Everyone seems in such a tearing hurry all the time. Not to mention the petrol fumes and general pollution, which is simply dreadful!'

'Yes, I've already heard your views on the Great Metropolis—about a million times!' Samantha retorted with a grin, suddenly realising just how much she'd needed the comfort of her sister's kind, warmly caring personality.

When Georgie had been born, and with two young children to look after as well as the baby, their mother had been rushed off her feet. Which was when her older sister had begun to loom large in Samantha's life. It was Edwina who'd picked her up when she'd fallen, wiped her tears when she was unhappy, and who throughout their earliest days at school had always protected and guarded her younger sister.

'So, how's work?' Edwina was saying. 'Busy as usual, I suppose?'

'You're quite right,' Samantha told her brightly, trying to put her own desperately upsetting worries aside for a moment. 'Incidentally, you're now looking at Minerva's new pension fund manager.'

Edwina beamed at her sister. 'Oh, darling! I'm *so* pleased. What a feather in your cap, to have got the job you wanted—and at such a young age.'

'I don't feel young.' Samantha grimaced. 'One more

year and I'll be thirty. Do you remember how we used to think that anybody over twenty-five was practically in their dotage?' she added with a wry smile, before asking how the shopping expedition had gone. 'Did you find everything you wanted?'

'No—nothing seemed to fit. I shall just have to go on a diet,' her sister told her gloomily. 'But not until after lunch, of course! And, since I arrived here early—and I knew that you'd be in a tearing hurry, as usual—I went ahead and ordered for both of us. Ah, here it comes now,' she added as a waiter approached their table. 'I chose one of your favourite starters—shrimps sizzling in hot garlic oil. I must say, it smells delicious!'

Normally very fond of the dish, Samantha could only stare down at her plate in dismay. The thought of eating even one mouthful was quite, quite beyond her.

'Are you feeling all right?' Edwina murmured, gazing at her sister with concern. She did look very pale and not at all her usual, bubbly self. 'If you don't want it we can always order something else. Maybe a salad would be a better choice? Or…'

'No, it's OK…' Samantha muttered, closing her eyes for a moment as she tried to ignore the strong, normally delicious aroma of garlic rising from the dish in front of her. 'I…er…I'm sorry, but I just don't think I can eat anything at the moment.'

'Darling—what's wrong?' Edwina frowned. 'You don't look at all well. Maybe you should see a doctor?'

Samantha could feel a dark bubble of hysterical laughter rising in her throat. 'I don't need to see a doctor!' she ground out through nervously clenched, chattering teeth. 'If…if you want to know the truth I've *already* s-seen one today. And…and apparently I'm g-going to have a b-baby,' she added, before suddenly bursting into tears.

'Oh, *Sam!*'

'I…I'm sorry….' she muttered, desperately searching

through her handbag for a tissue. 'I...I didn't mean to say anything...such a fool...in a restaurant of all p-places!'

'Who cares? They can just put up with it,' Edwina stated firmly, passing a large white handkerchief to the sobbing girl, before beckoning imperiously to a waiter and ordering a weak brandy and soda. 'Besides, no one can see us here, in the corner,' she added comfortingly. 'So, come on. Dry your tears—and tell me all about it.'

'Wh-what can I t-tell you?' Samantha sniffed, wiping her eyes and blowing her nose. 'I've been a stupid, careless fool. That's all there is to it.'

'Oh, really? I should think there is a lot more to it than that,' her sister murmured sceptically as the waiter returned to their table with the brandy and soda. 'Now, sip it slowly, and you'll feel a lot better.'

'How...how can you take this all so calmly?' Samantha asked, instinctively doing as she was told, and becoming aware that the nauseous feeling in her stomach was gradually subsiding.

Edwina smiled and shook her head. 'Darling—it's hardly the end of the world, you know. I...er...I'm assuming that it's Matt's baby, right?' And when her sister gave an unhappy, tearful nod she shrugged her shoulders. 'Well, I really don't see too many problems. You're both clearly mad about each other. So, what's to stop you getting married, and living happily ever after?'

'You...you simply don't understand!' Samantha wailed, before burying her face in the handkerchief once again. 'Oh, Lord—I'm not normally the sort of person who bursts into tears,' she added helplessly. 'I don't know what's come over me lately.'

'It's hormones, I'm afraid,' Edwina told her with a rueful smile. 'Now, exactly what is it that I don't understand? Because, believe me, there's *always* an answer to every problem.'

However, after she'd managed to persuade Samantha to explain fully the state of affairs in which she found herself, even she could see that there was no obvious, easy solution to what sounded a *very* complicated situation.

'Well, I think that you're just going to have to take one step at a time,' she said at last. 'And you're quite right. Because there's no doubt that the first thing you *must* do is have a long talk with Matt.'

'And just how do you suggest I do that? The damn man is thousands of miles away, in New York. And it's not exactly the sort of news one wants to tell anyone over the phone,' Samantha pointed out grimly, having by now managed to pull herself together. 'Besides, I've been walking all around London this morning, desperately trying to think this whole thing through. And got precisely nowhere!'

'Yes, but...'

'The facts are that Matt and I had an affair—which is now more or less over. He always made it crystal-clear that he just wanted a love affair—no commitment, no hassle. So, I tell him that I'm pregnant with his baby...and it's shock, horror all round. Will he wonder whether I'm blackmailing him into marriage? Yes, probably he will. And, even if he doesn't, he's going to feel obliged to do at least "the right thing" and support me and the child.'

'And so he should!' Edwina retorted firmly. 'It takes two people to make a baby. And he's got to face up to his responsibilities, whether he wants to or not.'

Samantha shook her head. 'You've lost sight of the main point. Which is all this ghastly business of the take-over battle. If I *do* tell him about the baby I'll have to give up my job. Because there's no way I can pretend that we aren't heavily involved with each other. On the other hand, our very brief affair is now over. Which means that if I don't name the father I can keep on working. And, as a single mother, it's going to be desperately important that I do so—if only to provide for my child.

'So, that's it, in a nutshell. To tell Matt—and lose my job. Or to keep silent, keep my job...and look after my baby.'

'Oh, darling! I...I simply don't know what to say...'

'Yeah, well, that makes two of us,' Samantha told her sister grimly. 'And, unless you can come up with an inspired solution to the problem, it looks as though it's going to be just about the hardest decision I'll ever have to take. And one which will have vital consequences for the rest of my life.'

CHAPTER SEVEN

IT HAD been the usual mad rush to get dressed and leave her apartment looking tidy.

What on earth was wrong with her these days? Samantha asked herself as she dashed out of her apartment building—before immediately recalling exactly what was 'wrong' with her. If this strange lethargy was a by-product of pregnancy, she really wasn't looking forward to the next seven months.

'I'm sorry to be late again this morning, Joe,' she muttered, tumbling breathlessly into the back of the waiting taxi. 'Unfortunately, I seem to have been making a habit of over-sleeping just lately.'

'It happens to us all, love.' The driver grinned at her in his mirror. 'I live out in Essex. So I have to be on the road really early, if I don't want to get caught up in all that commuter traffic. As my missus says...'

Taxi drivers were the same the world over, Samantha told herself with a sigh. Once they'd started on some long monologue, there was no stopping them. The easiest option was to lean back in her seat, close her eyes and allow the driver's words to flow over her head.

In any case, after all the emotional drama involved in yesterday's events, she was feeling just too exhausted to do any of her usual work in the cab. In fact, she couldn't even be bothered to open her newspaper. Which only went to show just how quickly she was going to pieces, since almost the first thing she normally did on waking, was to quickly review all the City news in the papers.

Unfortunately, the 'news' she'd been given yesterday

was far more important than anything she could read in the press, she told herself with another heavy sigh.

Goodness knows how she'd have got through the day if it hadn't been for Edwina, who'd proved to be such a wonderful tower of strength. Even when she'd behaved like an utter fool, and made such an idiot of herself in the restaurant, darling Edwina couldn't have been more kind or understanding.

Thank God for sisters! Ashamed of weeping so copiously over the other woman's broad, comfortable shoulder, she'd only put up a token resistance when her older sister had insisted on accompanying her out of the restaurant, and back to her loft apartment.

'Oh, come on, Sam! I'm certainly not leaving you on your own. Not for a few hours, anyway,' Edwina had said firmly, before marching into the apartment and going straight to the kitchen to make a soothing cup of tea.

'For one thing, it's obvious that you're still in a state of shock. And for another…well, I reckon you can do with a bit of female solidarity.' She grinned. 'My dear husband is a sweet, kind and lovely man, besides also being a doctor. But what he knows about how a woman *really* feels—and the emotional state we can sometimes get into when we're expecting a baby—could be written on the back of a postage stamp!'

'Thanks for being so kind and sweet to me,' Samantha murmured, gazing mistily at her older sister.

'Rubbish! That's what being part of a family is all about.'

'Yes, I suppose so. But the thing is… It's difficult to explain, but I seem to be emotionally all over the place at the moment.' Samantha frowned, trying to put into words the confused, nebulous feelings which seemed to have gripped her lately.

'What I really hate is not feeling fully in control of myself,' she ground out in exasperation, waving her hands distractedly in the air. 'For instance, I seem to be so bad-tempered, snapping at everyone for absolutely no reason. Quite honestly, there are times when I appear to be in danger of becoming totally paranoid about even the silliest things.'

Edwina laughed as she poured them both a cup of tea. 'I hate to tell you the truth, Sam, but that does sound very, *very* familiar!'

'You mean…it isn't just me? That it happens to other people—and I'm *not* going off my head?'

'Idiot! Of course you're not!' her sister quickly reassured her. 'Everyone's pregnancy is different, of course. But I'm sure you'll find that things will soon get better, as both you and the baby settle down together. In fact, being pregnant is really a very nice state to be in. Especially if you're like me,' she added with a grin. 'I know that "eating for two" is a load of nonsense. But, with my waistline expanding at a rate of knots, I found myself quite happily eating for three or four.'

'Oh, Lord!' Samantha groaned, staring at her sister in dawning horror. 'I'd forgotten all about how you used to stagger around with that huge bump, just before Rosie was born. Will I have to start letting out my waistbands straight away?' she muttered, gazing down at her flat stomach with dismay.

'Hey—calm down! There's some time to go before you're likely to notice any major changes,' Edwina told her firmly. 'Besides, you've got quite a different figure to mine. So, there could be a good chance that you could manage to be six or seven months pregnant before anyone really notices anything different about you.'

'Let's hope so!'

'Besides,' her sister pointed out, 'you've been earning a large salary. So, buying some really well-designed, expensive maternity outfits for the office won't be a problem.'

There was a long silence as they stared at one another, before Samantha said slowly, 'Talking of the office… It sounds as though you've come to the same conclusion as I have. That I'm going to have to keep on working at my job—right?'

Edwina gave a helpless shrug of her shoulders.

'I honestly don't know, Sam. I really am torn on this one. I mean, I've *always* believed that, if possible, it's far better for a child to have two parents. Because the life of a single mother is terribly, terribly hard. You've no idea, at the moment, just how desperately tired you're going to be,' she explained in a warm, sympathetic voice.

'I'm not saying it isn't possible to look after a baby on your own—because, of course, it is. Thousands of women go to work and bring up their children, with little or no help from anyone. But that doesn't mean to say that it's easy. Believe me, it's just about the hardest job there is.

'On the other hand...if telling Matt about the baby really and truly means that you won't be able to do your job, well...I just don't know. I'm sorry, darling,' Edwina added with another helpless shrug, 'I really *can't* help you with this decision—basically because I don't know what I would do in your shoes. I truly don't.'

Well, at least it was comforting to know that her sane, sensible and down-to-earth sister—who was also married to an equally well-adjusted doctor—had fully appreciated the almost impossible, difficult decision that she was going to have to make.

But now, as the taxi driver eventually came to the end of his long, interminable story, Samantha was beginning to wonder if, perhaps, everything wasn't *quite* so black and white as she had feared. Maybe she didn't have to rush into taking a decision straight away...?

If her sister was right, and there was going to be virtually no change in her figure for a few months—other than the fact that her breasts were already feeling hard and swollen—she could possibly leave taking any decision until after the take-over battle had been resolved.

In fact, just as long as she made certain that she had

absolutely *no* contact with Matt—in person or by phone—she could wait and see how the situation developed.

It was, perhaps, a cowardly way out of her current dilemma. But it *would* keep all her options open for as long as possible, she told herself, almost sagging with the relief at the prospect of not having to make such a desperately hard, difficult decision immediately.

Besides, she could recall one of the elderly professors, when she'd been at university, pointing out the folly of making snap judgements. 'Never decide anything in a hurry. Think hard and long—and then, if you can, put the problem aside for a while. In my experience,' he'd added with a twinkle in his faded blue eyes, 'I think you'll find that decisions have a way of making themselves.'

It was sage advice, Samantha told herself as the taxi slowed down outside her office block. And she'd do well to follow the guidance of such a clever and distinguished man.

Unfortunately, all her good intentions—not to mention her old professor's words of wisdom—seemed to fly straight out of the window approximately ten minutes after she'd entered her office.

'Hi!' Henry called out, bounding up to her desk. 'Seen the article in today's paper?' he added, slapping the pink newspaper down on the desk in front of her. 'It certainly looks like there's going to be a bit of a dog-fight, doesn't it?''

Although she'd been warned by her chairman, Samantha realised that she'd stupidly not prepared herself for the long, in-depth article, around which Henry had drawn a thick black circle.

Headed GOLIATH UNDER ATTACK FROM DAVID, the reporter had started by laying out, quite clearly, the situation between Matthew Warner's company and the smaller, English/French consortium which was seeking to take over Broadwood Securities.

In fact, the reporter seemed to have done a very good job, Samantha told herself, noting that he'd fairly explained the pros and cons of each company, before coming to the conclusion that it was going to be a very close decision as to who triumphed in the end.

As well as pointing out the obvious fact that the large holdings by pension fund managers were likely to swing the decision one way or the other, the reporter had also managed to get an interview with both the principals.

As one might have expected, the chairman of Kendal-Laval, while agreeing that they were a much smaller company, seemed confident of being able to persuade interested parties that their company was the best bet.

However, it was the interview with Matthew Warner which caused Samantha to catch her breath, and almost choke with suppressed rage and fury as the words seemed to leap from the page, burning into her brain with fiery letters as she read.

Matthew Warner, dynamic new Chief Executive of Broadwood, seems unperturbed by this threat to his empire.

'I welcome the challenge to prove that we are a strong company,' he said yesterday. 'I see no problem in persuading our shareholders where their best interest lies.'

However, when pressed to expand further on the subject, Mr Warner did confirm that he was not at all worried about the large blocks of shares held by the institutions. In fact, our reporter gained the distinct impression that Mr Warner believes he's already got their decision sewn up, in his favour.

Has he, even at this early stage in the battle, ensured that the largest block of shares, held by Minerva Utilities Management, will be pledged to support his company? If so—it could well mean that he's already home and dry.

'Good-looking guy—although he sounds a bit of an arrogant bastard, doesn't he?' Henry said, a note of admiration in his voice as he tapped a finger on the photograph of Matthew Warner which accompanied the article.

'You can say that again!' Samantha muttered through gritted teeth.

Almost shaking with rage, her head feeling as if it would explode with anger any minute, she stared down at the familiar features of the man who—*if there was any justice in this world!*—would one day prove to be too sharp for his own good—and give himself a very nasty cut on his own dagger.

Because Matt was virtually telling the world—through a highly respected City newspaper—that he'd already 'sweet-talked' the various pension fund managers into supporting him—and that his problems were all over, bar the shouting.

He was also making it pretty damn clear, to her at least, *exactly* what his motivation had been when he'd swept her so totally off her feet in New York.

Because he *must* have known about the threat of a take-over by then. And how could he make absolutely sure of winning the battle? Why—that was easy! All he had to do was to seduce one poor, stupid, deluded female—who, it just so happened, could swing the vote his way—make mad, passionate love to her and, hopefully, persuade the same stupid female that he and his company were absolutely the best thing since sliced bread. Right?

What was more…the rotten bastard might have just managed to get away with it, if she'd been less on the ball. Unfortunately, caught up by the pressure of business, he'd begun to neglect his victim, allowing her to 'wake up and smell the coffee'. And that, as he would soon discover, had been a bad, *bad* mistake.

I'll have his guts for garters! she promised herself vi-

ciously, before being recalled abruptly to the present as
Henry gave an embarrassed cough.

'I just thought I ought to mention... The fact is, I'm
not sure that I've been doing the right thing...' he muttered with an uncertain shrug of his shoulders.

'Oh, Henry—what on earth have you done *now*?' She
sighed heavily.

'Well, you see...the thing is...'

'Come on—spill the beans!' she ground out impatiently. 'Although if you've seduced the chairman's
daughter there's no way I can save your bacon. A case
of instant dismissal if ever I heard one!'

'How...how on earth did *you* find out?' he gasped,
staring at her as if he'd just seen a ghost.

'Oh, for heaven's sake—I was only joking,' she told
him with a grim laugh, before realising, from the sight of
his suddenly ashen face, that she had, quite inadvertently,
hit the nail on the head. 'You don't mean to say that you
actually have...?'

'I'm not saying *anything*!' he retorted, quickly recovering his usual aplomb.

'Very sensible,' she agreed tersely. 'It's a pity some
other people haven't followed such good advice!'

'Hmm...?' He frowned, not having any idea of what
she was talking about. 'Come again...?'

'Forget it!' she muttered, taking a deep breath and pulling herself together. 'Now, what were you trying to tell
me?'

'Ah...yes. Well, there were quite a lot of urgent phone
calls for you yesterday when you were away from the
office.'

'So...?'

'The thing is, Sam, they were all from Mr Matthew
Warner's offices, both in New York and here, in London.
They seemed to be wanting some sort of information,
and...well, I wasn't quite sure of exactly the right thing
to do,' he added hurriedly. 'So, after the first phone call,

I had them all transferred to my own office. And I just kept saying that you were away for the day. It just seemed a good idea…' His voice trailed away.

'You made *absolutely* the right decision, Henry,' she told him with a heartfelt sigh of relief. 'Well done!'

'So, you're not mad at me?'

'Far from it!' she assured him. 'However, I want you to make sure, from now on, that *all* calls from Mr Warner's offices are firmly blocked. It's *vitally* important that neither he nor anyone working for him ever gets through to me. Or anyone else in this department. Understand?'

'Well…sort of, I suppose. But it's hardly the end of the world if you do talk to his office, is it?'

'It would just about be the end of *my* world!' she retorted grimly.

'Look…there's nothing to stop him trying to have his case heard,' Samantha continued. 'In fact, I'd be surprised if he hadn't already hired a top-notch PR firm here in the UK, and started a huge public relations exercise. But absolutely *no one* in this department should talk to him on their own. Which is where taking any phone calls comes in.'

Henry sighed. 'It all seems very complicated.'

Samantha shook her head. 'No, it's really very simple. In the unlikely event, say, of Matthew Warner turning up to lay his case before us, our chairman would insist on there being *at least* two witnesses from either side, and fully recorded minutes taken of the meeting,' she explained patiently. 'That way, there could be no dispute about who said what, to whom—and absolutely *no* chance of anyone in this firm being suspected of either bribery or corruption.'

'Phew! That all sounds a bit heavy, doesn't it?'

'Not when you realise that there are many millions, if not *billions* of dollars at stake here, Henry,' she pointed out grimly. 'So, let's just concentrate on keeping our noses clean—and make sure we *never* take calls from Matthew Warner's offices—OK?'

'Oh, absolutely,' he agreed fervently, suddenly realising that this take-over battle wasn't just a game played between two companies, but involved an amazingly serious amount of money.

After Henry had left her office, Samantha tried to concentrate on the work in front of her, desperately trying to master her anger and disillusionment with Matt. It wasn't easy, but the sheer application of mental discipline, especially when dealing with vital matters concerning the finance of a company, gradually absorbed her full attention.

Deeply immersed in a page of complicated figures, she was slow to respond when Henry put his head around the door, muttering something about a press conference.

'Hmm...?' she muttered, not raising her eyes from the page in front of her.

'Come on, Sam!' he told her urgently. 'That guy— Matthew Warner? The girls in the back office tell me that CNN is just about to report a press conference which he's giving here in London.'

'Rubbish! He can't possibly be in London,' she snapped. 'Not when he's thousands of miles away in New York. Right?'

Henry shrugged. 'Suit yourself. I'm only passing on the message from some of the traders. They thought you might want to see what he's got to say.'

'You're right,' she acknowledged with a rueful shake of her head. 'I'm sorry, Henry,' she added, rising from her chair and walking across the room towards him. 'I do seem to have been giving you a hard time lately, don't I? But I suppose I'd better come along and see what the man has got to say for himself.'

'Yeah. It might be interesting,' Henry agreed blandly as she walked past him and on down the corridor.

Everyone, including his family, seemed to think that

he was pretty stupid. But even *he* was quite capable of seeing that any mention of Mr Warner was enough to bring his boss out in spots.

In fact, that guy ought to watch out! Henry thought, trailing after Samantha's slim figure into the dealing room, with its bank of Reuters' screens reporting stock movements across the world. Because Miss Thomas might be a beautiful, sexy woman, but she was also one very tough lady. And if Matthew Warner had managed to upset her in some way he really wouldn't like to be in the elegant shoes of the man, who was now being interviewed on a big screen tuned in to the lunchtime news edition of CNN.

'You seem to be taking things very calmly, Mr Warner,' a female reporter was saying. 'Aren't you at all worried about losing control of your large corporation?'

'I don't believe in taking anything for granted, of course,' Matt drawled, the camera zooming in for a head shot of the tall, handsome man sitting at his ease in the television studio. 'However, I do have to say that I am quietly confident of defeating this much smaller company. Which is one of the reasons why I flew into London yesterday.'

'Why London—as opposed to Paris or Bonn?'

'The City of London is very important to us,' he explained. 'We have our European headquarters here, of course, as well as large holdings in several merchant banks. And, being British myself,' he added, flashing a warm, charming smile at the camera, 'I couldn't resist the opportunity of visiting England in June.'

'That sounds interesting…' the interviewer probed. 'Are you hoping to have time to watch the tennis at Wimbledon?'

He grinned. 'Why not? I'm a great believer in mixing business with pleasure.'

'Yes, so I've heard!' The interviewer laughed. 'In fact,

I believe you gained quite a reputation, in the past, for being something of a playboy…?'

He shrugged his broad shoulders. 'As you say—that was very much in the past,' he drawled smoothly, clearly unruffled by the interviewer's comment.

'If they have any blood in their veins, most young men go through a brief period when they sow their wild oats and generally have a good time,' he continued, his green eyes beneath their heavy lids clearly glinting with amusement. 'Fortunately, however, it doesn't last very long. And, in my case, I'm frankly far too busy nowadays for any nonsense of that sort.'

'But you're not married…?' the female interviewer probed.

'No, I'm not,' he agreed coolly. 'Which, of course, means that I can give my whole and undivided attention to business matters. As I told you earlier…'

Watching as Matt smoothly turned the interview away from his own background, to concentrate on the issues at stake in the forthcoming boardroom battle, Samantha leaned against the wall, her arms folded protectively across her body as she concentrated on keeping her face entirely blank of all expression.

But it was almost impossible to do so, especially when she was practically grinding her teeth in overwhelming rage and fury. 'A great believer in mixing business with pleasure'…? *I'll say he is!* she fumed. And the damn man was *still* a playboy—whatever he might say to the contrary!

In fact, an overwhelming urge to scream out loud— denouncing the man on the screen in front of her as being a one hundred per cent dirty, rotten bastard—was proving to be almost irresistible.

It didn't help her iron control to hear snatches of conversation from two young, very pretty female colleagues standing close beside her. They, it seemed, were entirely captivated by the tall, dark and handsome figure of Broadwood's chief executive.

'Umm…*very* nice!' one girl was saying to the other. 'He may be a bit of a playboy businessman but what the heck? I'd be happy to play with *his* figures any night of the week!'

Her friend nodded in agreement. 'Yeah—I wouldn't be in a hurry to kick him out of *my* bed, either. I bet he's a real tiger between the sheets!' she added, before they both collapsed into muffled gales of laughter.

Well aware of the various covert glances being cast in her direction, Samantha struggled to maintain her composure. As far as her colleagues were concerned, this was possibly their first view of one of the two major contenders in the forthcoming take-over battle—and the first chance they'd had of catching a sight of him, in the flesh. So, there was bound to be considerable interest both in Matthew Warner and the reaction of their new head of department, Samantha Thomas.

You've got to act as though you've never seen this man before in your life, she told herself desperately, striving with all her might to maintain an expression of bland interest.

However, it was obviously important that she made absolutely sure all her colleagues and fellow workers got the message—loud and clear. They must have no doubt, at this stage of the game, that she had no intention of pre-judging the result.

'Well, that was very interesting,' she announced as the programme came to a close.

'Unfortunately…however much some females in this room might fancy their chances with the handsome Mr Matthew Warner…' she paused as a ripple of laughter ran around the room '…I'd like to remind everyone that he was, of course, speaking at his *own* press conference. Where he would, quite naturally, be putting the best possible spin on the situation as it stands at present.

'However, not only have we yet to hear or see anything from the other side, but it is still early days. There's a long way to go before we finally come to an impartial decision. So, let's get back to work and concentrate on the issues, not on the personalities—or the looks—of the two chairmen.'

Feeling satisfied and heartened by the general murmur of agreement from her colleagues, Samantha turned and walked quickly back into her office.

Closing the door, she sagged back against it as she took a deep, shuddering sigh. Eventually managing to pull herself together, although her whole body was still shaking with suppressed rage and fury, she walked over to sit down at her desk.

Right! It was all now as clear as the nose on her face. There could be no doubt—no doubt at all. Matt had used her; abused her trust—and hadn't even had the good manners to let her know when he was coming to London. So, there was going to be no need for her to spend hours and hours wondering whether she was doing the right thing in not telling him about her pregnancy. No child of *hers* would want a father like *him*—that's for sure, she told herself grimly.

However, as the afternoon progressed, she was finding it harder and harder to keep her anger at white-hot level. For one thing, it didn't achieve anything. And, for another, she was just feeling so damn miserable...and upset...and unhappy that, if she hadn't needed this job to support her unborn baby, she'd have thrown in the towel right that minute—and walked away from the whole awful mess.

But of course, like all bad dreams, the day finally came to an end.

'How about joining me for a meal tonight?' Henry asked, coming into her office just as she was snapping shut the lock on her briefcase.

Samantha shook her head. 'Thanks for the offer. But

I'm feeling absolutely bushwhacked. So, I'm just planning to go home, have a hot meal and then a long bath—before hitting the sack!'

'I'm not feeling exactly bright-eyed and bushy-tailed myself,' he agreed as they walked down the corridor and entered the elevator. 'It's been a long day. But I thought that guy, Matthew Warner, did put up a good case for supporting his firm.'

'It was just a PR exercise,' Samantha told him firmly as the elevator doors opened and they walked out through the main foyer, on to the pavement outside the office building.

'It's easy to be swayed by a professional piece of propaganda. So take care to remind yourself that that's all it was,' she warned him.

'Don't worry—I've got the message.' Henry grinned, slipping an arm around her waist and giving her a brief kiss on the cheek. 'I just wish you'd get mine!'

'Oh, Henry! I've told you, I don't know how many times…'

'Don't! Don't kill my hopes, Carlotta!' he suddenly declared in loud, dramatic tones, clutching his hands to his heart as he knelt down on one knee, on the pavement in front of her. 'How can you be so cruel? How can you blight my hopes like this?' he cried. 'Surely you must know that I am yours to command—even to the ends of the earth?'

'For heaven's sake!' Samantha hissed, her face flaming with embarrassment as several passers-by stopped to view the scene taking place on the pavement.

'Yes! That's what I want—just a slice of heaven!' Henry continued, clearly having the time of his life in portraying the hero of some oddball Victorian melodrama. 'Don't spurn my hand and my heart, Carlotta—for I have no future without you!'

'Damn right! There's certainly no future *for* you if you don't put a stop to this dreadful performance right now!'

Samantha retorted with a grin, abandoning the struggle not to respond to Henry's gales of infectious laughter as he finally abandoned his dramatic stance of a rejected suitor.

'Relax—I was only teasing,' he said, standing up and brushing the pavement dust from his trousers. 'You aren't *really* going to sack me, are you?'

'No, of course not—you idiot!' she told him. 'But, all the same,' she added, before turning to walk away, 'I think you'd better concentrate on the day job, Henry. Because that was quite the worst piece of acting I've ever seen. And if you ever dare call me Carlotta again I'll *definitely* tell the chairman the name of the man who seduced his daughter!' she threw over her shoulder, leaving Henry still laughing as she strode swiftly down the street.

Honestly! Was Henry a case for psychiatric treatment—or what? she asked herself ruefully, while keeping a lookout for a passing taxi. However, maybe it might be a good idea to have him transferred to another department, just for the time being? Not just because he'd been acting the fool right outside the office just now, but because she still had reservations about Henry's ability to keep himself out of trouble during the take-over. And she was sufficiently fond of the silly guy to make sure that, even if he was incapable of protecting himself, he was safely tucked out of harm's way.

Besides…although Henry had only been kidding, just now, she was well aware of the fact that he would, given half a chance, like to extend their current work relationship into a more personal one. And, since she wasn't interested in either Henry or…

Hearing the sound of an engine behind her, Samantha turned, half raising her hand to hail the vehicle, should it prove to be a taxi. Slightly disappointed to note that it was merely a long black limousine, she continued walking along the pavement, not taking any particular notice when the limo came to a halt on the road just in front of her.

The next few moments seemed to pass in a sudden blur as the rear passenger door opened, a man jumped out and she found herself suddenly swept off her feet—before being unceremoniously dumped in the back of the vehicle.

'What…what's going on?' she cried out in alarm, as soon as she managed to catch her breath. 'And…and just *what* do you think you're doing?' she added, her dazed vision clearing to see Matthew Warner seating himself down beside her, slamming the passenger door shut and instructing his driver to 'get a move on'!

'Who was that crazy guy?' Matt demanded angrily, quickly pressing a button and closing the partition dividing them from his driver. 'And what the hell did he think he was doing—kissing you and playing the fool outside your office just now?'

'It was only Henry Graham fooling around,' she muttered, struggling to sit up on the seat, her cheeks flushed as she quickly pulled down the short, straight skirt of her navy blue suit, which had risen well up her thighs. 'Much more to the point,' she continued through gritted teeth, 'I want to know what *you* think you're doing, kidnapping me like this.'

Matt merely shrugged his broad shoulders. 'It seemed the only way of us managing to have a few words together. You have, after all, refused to answer or return my phone calls to your apartment—and blocked all my attempts to contact you at your office.'

The mention of her office suddenly brought Samantha sharply back down to earth.

'You must be out of your mind!' she gasped, sinking as low as she could against the leather upholstery seat. 'If anyone sees us together, I'm in deep, *deep* trouble,' she muttered fearfully, well aware that it would only take one quick, brief sighting of her and Matt together at this delicate stage of his take-over battle, and she would immediately lose her job.

'We must *not* be seen anywhere near each other at the moment. Surely you know that?' she demanded curtly. '*You* may not care what happens to me—but I sure as hell do!'

'Yes, of course I know the risks,' he told her impatiently. 'But they're very small. And, besides, I have no intention of discussing any business with you. This, I can assure you, my dear Samantha,' he added menacingly, 'is strictly personal!'

'I'm not interested in any personal relationship with you,' she grated, not looking at him as she quickly surveyed the interior of the car, realising with a sigh of relief that the smoked-glass windows would prevent anyone outside from viewing the occupants within. 'Kindly ask your driver to stop—and let me out of here, right this minute!' she added icily, sliding forward in her seat and reaching down towards her handbag and briefcase, lying scattered on the floor of the vehicle.

His swift response caught her completely by surprise as he quickly grasped her by the arm, roughly pulling her towards him.

'What do you think you're doing?' she cried, a jagged shaft of fear shivering down her backbone as she stared up at his tanned face, the green eyes glinting chips of ice, his wide mouth set and grim as his arms tightened about her trembling body.

'I need to talk to you—and I need to talk to you *now!*' he told her firmly.

Rapidly recovering from the shocking suddenness of his movement, Samantha was by now almost spitting with fury. Bringing up her hands and placing them firmly against his chest, she tried to lever herself away from his embrace, which seemed to be tightening around her like a band of steel.

'I...I don't want to talk to you,' she panted breathlessly, her puny strength no match for his superior strength as she found herself crushed against his hard, firm chest.

Unbelievably, because there was absolutely *nothing* funny about this situation, she heard him give a low rumble of laughter.

'If you won't talk to me,' he drawled sardonically, 'I shall just have to think of some other way to pass the time, won't I?'

'Oh, no!' she cried out hurriedly. 'No! Absolutely not…no…!'

But it was no good. Her protests were abruptly silenced as he swiftly lowered his dark head, pressing his mouth firmly to her lips.

Frantically beating her fists against his broad shoulders had simply no effect at all. He took not a blind bit of notice of her actions, and it was doubly humiliating to realise that the lips possessing her own were not, as she had feared, subjecting her to a hard, brutal kiss. They were, alas, soft and warm and tender as they moved sensually over her own trembling mouth, only too easily arousing a response she was unable to control as a treacherous warmth invaded her body.

It simply wasn't fair! was almost her last, despairing thought as she seemed unable to prevent herself from surrendering to the sweet seduction of his lips and tongue. Because she really *had* done her best to keep away from this man; to purge him ruthlessly both from her life and her own, private thoughts. And yet there seemed to be nothing she could do to combat the sexual chemistry which had always been such a very strong, powerful force in their relationship.

Even as she trembled in his arms, unable to stop herself from feverishly responding to his increasing ardour, she knew…in her heart of hearts…that Matt was quite deliberately using the one weapon against which he must know she was defenceless. But, it was two long weeks since he'd held her like this. And there was nothing she could do to prevent all her carefully erected defences from falling away, one by one, and leaving her a helpless prisoner amidst the rising tide of passion now flooding through her veins.

CHAPTER EIGHT

'IF YOU don't mind me saying so, Sam, you're looking a bit rough this morning.'

'Well, I'd rather not have it pointed out *quite* so bluntly, Henry! But I do have to admit that you're probably right,' Samantha admitted with a heavy sigh. 'In fact, "rough" is just about the perfect description of how I feel at the moment.'

'Would a cup of coffee help?' he asked, gazing down with concern at the girl's pale face, and the deep shadows beneath her normally sparkling blue eyes.

Samantha nodded. 'That would be great,' she admitted, waiting until he'd left the room before slumping back in her chair behind the desk and wishing, with all her heart, that she could go to sleep for a hundred years.

She wouldn't normally have had any problem in recognising that the cataclysmic row with Matt yesterday was bound to have left her feeling extremely upset and unhappy. And such strong feelings could often, of course, produce symptoms of stress and strain in one's body.

Unfortunately, this pregnancy of hers was suddenly making everything far more complicated. How was she supposed to know whether the fact that she'd been dreadfully sick earlier this morning was merely due to the fact that she was expecting a baby—or was a result of the deeply upsetting confrontation in Matt's limousine? That bitter clash between them—so quickly followed by the devastating effect he always seemed to have on her—had left her feeling so totally shattered that she'd barely been able to get a wink of sleep all night.

The return of Henry with not only a cup of hot coffee

but also a tall glass of cold water successfully managed to distract her, for a few moments at least, from the tangled, chaotic mess which she seemed to have made of her private and business life.

Unfortunately, after he'd once again left her office—and despite all her efforts to immerse herself in work—there seemed nothing she could do to clear the dark, satanic vision of Matt's handsome face and strong body from her tired mind.

Since he was much taller and stronger than herself, *and* had virtually kidnapped her from the middle of a pavement—in broad daylight, for heaven's sake!—it really hadn't been her fault when she'd found herself clasped so tightly in his arms, in the back of that large limousine. She'd clearly been the victim of both his sneaky behaviour and overwhelming strength. So, there was no way she could be blamed for anything, up to that point—right?

Unfortunately, things had begun to go disastrously wrong from that moment onwards. In fact, only a few nanoseconds after his lips had touched hers, the seemingly 'helpless victim' had apparently had an immediate attack of amnesia, completely and utterly forgetting that she was, supposedly, feeling nothing but deep anger against the man in question.

Equally unfortunate, alas, was the fact that, far from screaming blue murder and struggling to escape her fate, she'd more than willingly succumbed to the hot surge of erotic excitement shuddering through her trembling body, responding without conscious thought as she'd savoured the warm, sensual touch of his lips on hers, and the clear arousal of the hard, muscular frame pinning her ruthlessly back against the leather upholstery.

Once again, as had happened in New York, it seemed as though they had both, quite clearly, taken complete leave of their senses. In fact, it probably wasn't too much of an exaggeration to describe their behaviour as stark, staring mad.

But, of course, it was easy enough to view what had happened in retrospect. At the time, with the claustrophobic atmosphere within the tightly enclosed, confined space suddenly becoming highly charged with an ever-increasing, potent mixture of sexual desire and sheer lust, she'd found herself a helpless prisoner of her own mounting passion.

Pulsating waves of heat had seemed to scorch through every part of her body, her senses at fever-pitch as she'd heard him cursing under his breath whilst trying to undo the tiny pearl buttons of her white silk blouse, before impatiently tugging the thin silk from beneath her waistband, and groaning with pleasure as he was at last able to run his hands over her soft, bare flesh.

'God—you're so lovely!' he muttered thickly, the husky note in his voice and the feel of his warm fingers sweeping up over her skin to close enticingly over her full breasts finally causing her emotions to spin completely out of control.

And the really awful, totally disgraceful fact was that she simply hadn't cared! She hadn't given two hoots about the fact that she'd been lying half naked within Matt's arms in the back of a limousine which, at that precise moment, was being driven slowly through the crowded streets of London.

How could she? Samantha's cheeks now burned with shame and deep mortification. How *could* she have behaved in such an absolutely disgraceful, utterly wanton manner? However, at the time it had seemed as though she'd been totally gripped by a strangely languorous, yielding and timeless force, which drove out all fear of the past and the future. The only truth…the only reality…had seemed to be the overwhelming need to respond to his mounting ardour, and a compelling urge to offer up her body for his delight.

She'd been totally seduced by the feel of his warm mouth and hands on her bare flesh as he'd gently caressed

the soft curves of her full breasts; it had been the rough
texture of his tongue flicking erotically over one of her
tautly swollen, newly tender nipples that had prompted
her to give an involuntary cry of painful discomfort—and
which had sharply brought her down to earth, and back
into the real world.

'Darling…what's wrong?' he muttered hoarsely, raising his dark head and gazing down with concern at the
girl in his arms. 'I didn't mean to hurt you, sweetheart…'
he added, dimly aware that those wonderfully exciting,
deliciously soft breasts of hers did seem to be much fuller
and larger than he'd remembered.

But Samantha wasn't listening. Shuddering with self-
disgust at her utterly shameless, wanton behaviour, she
immediately began trying to push him away.

'Leave me alone!' she gasped breathlessly, a deep
crimson flush rising over her pale cheeks as she struggled
to sit up, cursing violently under her breath as she tried
to readjust her clothing. But she couldn't seem to control
her trembling, nervous fingers, and she had to suffer the
ultimate, humiliating embarrassment of having to allow
Matt to refasten her bra, before he slowly and carefully
helped to tuck her blouse back into the waistband of her
skirt.

'I'm sorry. I shouldn't have got carried away like that.'
He sighed heavily, his words accompanied by a rueful
shake of his dark head. 'In fact, I ought to have known
what was likely to happen. Every time I intend having a
long, serious talk with you we always seem to end up
making love instead.'

'Speak for yourself!' she snapped, hurriedly attempting
to do something about her long, heavy straight hair which,
during their torrid embrace, had tumbled down from its
original neat knot on the top of her head, and was now
lying in a tangled mass about her shoulders.

He gave a short bark of sardonic laughter. 'Oh, yes, I
was indeed speaking for myself. And for you, too,

Samantha,' he drawled, raising a hand and firmly grasping her chin, before turning her face towards him. 'It takes two to tango—doesn't it?'

Trying to tear her gaze away from the intense, searching light of those granite-hard, emerald-green eyes of his, she could feel her face flaming with embarrassment. Unfortunately, Matt was absolutely right. They were both victims of this quite unaccountable and amazingly strong force, which she seemed completely unable to combat.

'OK...OK,' she admitted through nervously chattering teeth, before jerking her head away and turning to stare out of the window. 'But this is where the music has to stop—at once, and for ever.

'I'm not going to rehash what has happened between us. We both know the score,' she continued bitterly, still keeping her back to him as she addressed his shadowy reflection in the dark glass windows. 'I now know exactly *why* you came on to me like a heat-seeking missile in New York. And if I got temporarily swept off my feet...?' She shrugged her slim shoulders. 'Well, I've got no one else to blame but myself. However, I've now seen the light, and it's all over—right?'

'No, it's most decidedly not "right",' he growled impatiently. 'Principally, because I don't have the slightest idea of what you're talking about. Surely you can't think...'

Swiftly gathering up her handbag and her briefcase, Samantha took a deep breath and turned around to face him.

'Do me a favour!' she snapped tersely through gritted teeth. 'I'm sick and tired of playing games with you, Matt. But you've no need to worry. I'm perfectly capable of being ultra-professional; of taking a calm, considered and, above all, an *impartial* decision about whether or not your bloody company wins the forthcoming take-over battle.

'But that's *it*! So, you can now relax—and leave me

alone,' she added, before she realised that the limousine had come to a halt.

Quickly glancing out through the window, she noted that they were stalled at some road works in Park Lane. And she suddenly knew what she had to do. Reaching forward, she quickly pressed down the door handle, opening the passenger door and leaping out on to the road in one, fluid movement.

Spinning around to face him, she grated, 'I don't ever want to see you again, you…you corrupt bastard! So get lost—and stay lost!' she added, slamming the door shut and running back down the road to hail a passing taxi.

But now, as she leaned her elbows on the desk, weakly resting her tired, sore head in her hands, Samantha found not a scrap of satisfaction in yet again recalling yesterday's events. Because they had, after all, been running continuously through her head during the past twelve hours.

It was one thing to tell someone that you never wanted to see them again—and quite another to have to face the result of your action.

Initially, on finally reaching her apartment, she'd been buoyed up by the sheer adrenaline and fury racing through her mind and body, following her confrontation with Matt. However, as the evening had worn on, and she'd managed to calm down somewhat, she'd finally realised what never seeing him again was *really* going to mean to her. And the belated discovery of her true feelings had brought nothing in its train but wormwood and gall.

Because what she now knew, without the slightest shadow of doubt, was that once again she'd made the utterly disastrous mistake of falling deeply in love with Matthew Warner.

How could she have been such a fool? To have badly burnt her fingers once was perfectly understandable. It happened to people all the time. But to allow it to happen

yet again—nine years later—had been the absolute height
of folly. And, almost worst of all, she'd got no one to
blame but herself.

It didn't seem to matter that he'd quite callously used
her for his own ends. No matter how much she might
fight against it, he was the man with whom she'd first
fallen madly and deeply in love—and it seemed that now,
all these years later, she was still deeply in thrall to that
strong emotion. Quite simply, he wasn't just the father of
her baby—he was, whether she liked it or not, the one
true love of her life.

Any hope that by burying herself in work she might
somehow manage to alleviate the bitter torment in her
mind, or the desperate, aching need of her body for his,
seemed to have absolutely no effect on Samantha's tor-
tured emotions. In fact, her temper was on such a short
fuse lately that she was becoming fed up with having to
apologise to Henry for continually being such a grouch.

The only thing which seemed to have kept her even
halfway sane had been the wise counsel and sympathetic
support of her older sister.

'Oh, Lord—what is it now?' Edwina had laughed on
answering the phone yesterday. 'Did you ring your doctor
about taking folic acid for the first three months of your
pregnancy?'

'Yes, I did. Unfortunately, she seemed a bit miffed,
because it was already on the list she'd given me, when
I first went to see her,' Samantha had said, sighing at her
own stupidity. 'Quite frankly, I was in such a state that
day that I've only just got around to reading about all the
things I should and shouldn't do. Which is why I'm ringing you,' she'd added, picking up the piece of paper in
front of her and frowning at what seemed an incredibly
long list of instructions for pregnant women. 'It all seems
a bit much. No alcohol...hardly any coffee—'

'I'm sorry, love,' Edwina had interrupted her quickly. 'I really must go. Georgie's just arrived.'

'What on earth is she doing, driving around the country in the middle of the week? If she doesn't watch it she'll lose her job.'

'Tell me about it!' her older sister had groaned. 'Unfortunately, it's too late, because she *has* lost her job, once again. Apparently, Georgie's last boss got fed up with her saying she was too busy to come into work on a Friday.'

'You're kidding…? Even Georgie couldn't be that daft.'

'Oh, yes, she could.' Edwina had laughed. 'It seems her boss said he wasn't interested in hearing any excuses about her need for long weekends—and promptly sacked her on the spot. So, she's now feeling very sorry for herself, and has come down to stay with me for a few days, to lick her wounds. Although she's almost bound to get yet another job straight away.'

Samantha had shaken her head in wry amusement. 'Knowing Georgie, I'm quite sure she will.'

'I must go, darling. The silly cuckoo is leaning against the doorbell and the noise is deafening. I'll call you tomorrow.'

It was only after her sister had put down the phone that Samantha had realised she hadn't warned Edwina about saying nothing to Georgie about the baby. However, she had enough to worry about—without adding Georgie to the list. Besides, it was hardly a subject which was likely to interest her younger sister.

Although she loved her dearly, Samantha had no illusions that Georgie was anything but a social butterfly. Tall, slim, with dark blonde curly hair and an amazing figure, Georgie wafted through life on what seemed a pink, rosy cloud, totally undisturbed by and unheeding of the sometimes grim, difficult facts of existence in this day and age. Still, she was very young. There was plenty of time for her to get a rather firmer grip on life. Although that would, perhaps, be rather a pity, since Georgie, for all her faults, brought a great deal of enjoyment and happiness into many people's lives.

As the days went by, it seemed that Matt had definitely got the message. Unfortunately, realising she would never see him again did not seem to have made her life any easier, Samantha told herself grimly as she prepared for bed one evening.

Even when she'd stood under the shower, getting ready to go to the office this morning, shampooing her hair and defiantly whistling a tune from an old musical—'I'm going to wash that man right out of my hair'—she'd known that she wasn't fooling anyone, let alone herself. The man in question seemed to have pervaded her very soul, and she very much feared that there was no way she would ever be able to totally root out either Matt, or his dark image, from her life in the future.

'Never mind, kid—you and I will just have to get along without him, won't we?' she said now, addressing her unborn baby as she removed her cool summer dress and stood in front of the mirror in her bedroom, regarding her slender figure clothed only in an ivory silk and lace teddy—and wondering just how soon she could expect to wave goodbye to her slim waist.

Talking to her baby was something which she'd found herself doing increasingly over the past few days. She hadn't, of course, any idea whether it was likely to be a boy or a girl. And, although it was apparently possible to learn in advance the sex of one's baby, she still couldn't quite make up her mind whether to find out—or wait and see what arrived in seven months' time.

However, she was finding it increasingly comforting to have long, involved conversations with her as yet unborn child. Only in the privacy of her own home, of course, she reminded herself quickly, before sinking slowly down on to the bed, and giving way to a few weak tears of self-pity.

'Well…if you can't cry in the privacy of your own bedroom, where can you?' she muttered out loud, fiercely blowing her nose and trying to pull herself together. Talking to yourself was definitely one of the first signs of madness. Although whether talking to her baby also came under that heading she wasn't quite sure…

Just about to change into her nightgown and climb into bed, she was suddenly disturbed by the shrill ringing of her front-door bell.

Oh, no! She'd completely forgotten that she had asked Henry to send around by courier some papers which she needed for an early meeting tomorrow morning. But, after a quick glance down at her watch, Samantha realised that it was highly unlikely such a service would be operating at this hour in the evening. Unless…unless, of course, Henry had decided to deliver them in person?

With a heavy sigh, she slipped on a thin blue silk gown, before walking swiftly through the dark sitting room towards the front door.

It was only much later that she cursed herself for not having the sense to look through the eye-hole, set in her door, to check exactly *who* was outside on the landing. How many times had she thought, Silly fool, when reading about cases of single women carelessly opening their front doors to prowlers? And yet there she'd been, taking the same, incredibly stupid action.

'Honestly, Henry—it's really far too late…' she said now, not thinking as she opened the door, and putting out a hand for the file of papers.

But it wasn't Henry. There was no file of papers. Only the tall, clearly angry figure of Matthew Warner.

Contemptuously ignoring her puny efforts as she quickly tried to shut the door in his face, he walked firmly and purposefully past her through the small hall, and into the large sitting room.

'What are you doing here?' she cried, swiftly closing the door before running into the sitting room after him.

'And just *who* is Henry?' Matt demanded angrily.

'What?' She stared across the darkened room at him, momentarily confused by Matt's sudden appearance. 'Henry Graham? He's not important. Just someone I work with, that's all,' she muttered impatiently, having far more important things on her mind than the identity of her assistant.

'Hmm…it certainly looks as though Henry was going to get *really* lucky tonight!' Matt drawled with heavy sarcasm as she hurried across the room to switch on a lamp.

'I don't know what you're talking about,' she snapped. 'And just what the hell do you think you're doing, bursting in here at this time of night? I thought I told you to get lost!'

'Yes, I can see it might be just a *little* awkward,' he drawled sardonically, ignoring her words as he nodded towards the open door of the bedroom, the soft light from her bedside lamp flooding through into the darker area of the sitting room. 'Nice little love nest you've got here, sweetheart! Perfect for entertaining tired businessmen, such as myself, or the unknown Henry, or…' he shrugged '…any lucky man who just happens to call by—right?'

Still shocked by his sudden appearance, Samantha took some moments to comprehend fully the meaning behind the harsh, cruelly drawled words echoing around the room—which was still mostly shrouded in darkness, other than the small pool of light provided by the lamp she'd just switched on.

'How dare you? How *dare* you insinuate that I…that I would even…?' Words failed her as she glared at him.

'My dear Samantha—I wouldn't dream of insinuating anything at all. Surely the evidence speaks for itself?'

Having by now taken a deep breath, and partially pulled herself together, Samantha realised that it was pointless to indulge in a slanging match with this man. If he wished to think of her as some sort of light, promiscuous woman, that was his problem, not hers.

Unfortunately, as so often happened in real life, it was easy enough to come to a swift, rational decision—but very hard, not to say almost impossible, to keep to it under extreme provocation.

Goodness knows what Matt thought he was doing here, but it *was* her home—and he *was* invading her own, personal space. So, the sooner she got rid of this tense, frighteningly sensual atmosphere which always seemed to crackle like electricity between them, the better.

'I don't know, or care, why you're here,' she said firmly, putting her thoughts into action as she moved slowly and purposefully around the room, turning on all the lamps. And it clearly was an improvement, she told herself as the atmosphere immediately seemed to lighten, in direct ratio to the amount of light now clearly illuminating the large space.

'I'm here simply because there's a lot of unfinished business between us,' he said slowly, beginning to pace up and down the room. 'I don't know what's got into your head. Quite frankly, I've never understood how women think, in any case,' he added with a harsh bark of laughter.

'Just another plain, ordinary, everyday male chauvinist pig!' she grumbled angrily to herself.

'What…?' he demanded, spinning around on his heel.

'Oh…nothing,' she muttered, hugging her arms protectively about herself as she leaned back against a long, slim Swedish sideboard bearing a drinks tray, the telephone and a large file of papers on which she'd been working earlier in the evening.

As always, the damned man was looking diabolically attractive. Now that the room was properly lit, she was able to see that he'd clearly come here from some official City function, since he was wearing a black dinner jacket over long, slim black trousers. His white evening shirt caused his tanned face to appear even darker than usual, the shadows of the room throwing his high cheekbones into sharp relief.

A long silence fell over the room, the only sound being the faint rumble of traffic and the occasional toot of a horn down in the street far below.

Try as she might, Samantha couldn't seem to tear her eyes away from his tall, dominant figure. Every one of the physical sensations she experienced whenever she was alone with Matt now returned to assail her more fiercely than ever. Why was it that only with him should she feel her heart pounding so rapidly, her flesh burning and then shivering, as if she had a fever, her ears almost deafened by the sound of the blood racing around her body?

This man had quite deliberately used her for his own ends, she told herself fiercely. It was just possible he hadn't known, but he certainly wouldn't care, if her close involvement with him meant that she could lose her job. And, while he wasn't of course corrupt—an accusation which she'd made the other day in the heat of the moment—he was certainly a *very* sharp businessman. Perfectly willing to sacrifice everyone and everything to gain his own ends.

And yet…and yet, even after laying out the case against him, point by point, she knew that it had been an ultimate disaster to have become involved with Matt once again. Because she knew, with absolute certainty, that he was the first and the last love of her life. And calling him all the names under the sun didn't seem to have the slightest effect on her emotions. Quite simply—she loved him.

But she had to be strong. Strong and firm—both with him and herself. The sooner she got him out of this apartment—and out of her life—the better it would be, both for herself and her unborn child.

'OK, what do you want to talk about?' she queried coldly, resolutely forcing herself to ignore the dark attraction of the man who was now standing at one of the floor-to-ceiling windows, gazing out at the dark evening sky and the twinkling lights of the surrounding buildings.

'I'm not quite sure where to begin,' he said, slowly turning around to face her. 'I haven't been able to see you before now quite simply because I've been so damned busy. This take-over seems to be taking over my whole life at the moment,' he sighed, brushing a tired hand through his thick dark hair.

There was another long silence as she stared across the room at him, before she took a deep breath. 'You're bigger and heavier than I am. So, it doesn't look as if I can stop you talking about anything you like. However, there's no way I'm prepared to listen to one word about your take-over battle. Surely I made my position quite clear the last time we met?'

'Ah, yes. I have no problem in remembering your ''position'' in the limousine,' he drawled, his green eyes glinting with sardonic amusement.

Even from the other side of the room, he could see the deep crimson flush rising swiftly over her pale cheeks. 'And very nice it was, too!' he added, clearly enjoying twisting the knife in the wound, and causing her the maximum amount of embarrassment.

'You really are the pits—aren't you?' she grated bitterly. 'I don't see why I should have to listen to any more of this nonsense,' she added, turning her back on him and reaching for the bottle of malt whisky on the drinks tray. Despite anything her doctor might say, if ever there was a time that called for a slug of strong alcohol—this was clearly it!

'If you're pouring yourself a glass of whisky, I'll have one too.' His voice, suddenly coming from just behind her shoulder, caused her to almost jump out of her skin with fright.

She'd never known anyone to move so quickly as he did, she thought, her hands shaking almost uncontrollably as she tried to unscrew the top of the bottle. Slow, silent...and as lethal as a panther, she thought wildly.

A sudden rush of fear and panic that she would weaken, that she wouldn't be able to maintain her defiant stance much longer, lent a savage edge to her voice as she snapped, 'I'd much prefer to ram the bottle down your beastly throat. But it doesn't look as if I've got any choice in the matter, does it?'

'Bitch!' he growled angrily as he grasped her arm, roughly spinning her around to face him. 'What is it with you, lady? God knows, I've done my best to keep our relationship going. In fact, it could possibly be said that I've neglected my own business to do so. And all I get...' he added furiously, putting his hands on her shoulders and giving her a rough shake. 'All I get from you is nothing but hard words. What's wrong with you, Samantha?'

She gave a snort of bitter laughter. 'There's absolutely nothing wrong with *me*!' she ground out angrily. 'At least *I've* been straightforward and honest!'

He frowned down at her. 'And just what the hell is that supposed to mean?'

'Oh, come on!' She gave a shrill, angry laugh. 'Do I *really* have to spell it out for you?'

'One of the reasons I'm here tonight is because you were throwing some pretty wild, serious allegations of corrupt behaviour at me the last time we met. So, yes,' he drawled icily, 'I really think you *will* have to spell out exactly what's going on in that complicated brain of yours. Because, quite frankly, it seems to have blown a fuse somewhere along the line.'

Cold shivers feathered down her spine at the tone of grim menace in his voice. The sooner she brought this disastrous confrontation to a close the better.

'There's nothing wrong with *my* brain! However, if you want me to spell it out in words of one syllable, I'll be quite happy to do so,' she ground out, her blue eyes flashing with anger as she related, step by step, the underhand methods he'd used in the hope of gaining her co-operation, and thus ensuring he would win his take-over battle.

'Unfortunately for you, it's all been a complete waste of time,' she finished caustically as he remained staring silently and grimly down at her, not having said a word during her precise, detailed account of all that had happened over the past two months. 'I am quite capable of taking a professional view. I and my team will come to an impartial decision, without fear or favour. And I will *not* be swayed by anything you might say or do!'

Shivering with nervous tension, she instinctively braced herself to receive a loud, violent denial of all his misdeeds. And therefore was astonished when, after a long silence following her angry words, he merely gave a short bark of sardonic laughter.

'I've heard some strange tales in my time, Sam—but I guess that totally paranoiac fantasy of yours really takes the biscuit!' he told her with grim amusement, his shoulders still shaking with laughter. 'The whole scenario is complete moonshine—and well you know it.'

'It's not moonshine. It's the *truth*!'

'But I particularly like that statement of yours about not being influenced by anything I might say or do,' he continued, completely ignoring her heated protest. 'If what you're saying is true, it doesn't look as though I've got anything to lose—does it?'

Staring up at him in confusion, she became aware that the expression in his glittering, hard green eyes seemed to be changing. Growing cloudy and opaque, they conveyed a message which she *did* understand, only too well, as it triggered a subconscious response deep in her body.

The hands clasping her shoulders seemed to tighten, the fingers clenching involuntarily and biting into her soft flesh as he took a half-step forward, pinning her firmly to both the hard wooden sideboard and his equally hard, firm torso.

Through the thin silk of her gown, she could feel the way his heart was pounding, echoing her own wild pulse beats. As his fingers relaxed their cruel grip and began sliding down over her back to encircle her body, her nostrils were filled with the sharp, astringent aroma of his cologne, his face now so close to her own that she could see every pore, every indentation of his tanned skin and the hard line of his mouth, moving with infinite slowness down towards her trembling lips.

Yet once again, as always with this man, it seemed as if she had become mentally paralysed. Her lips, which should have only opened to denounce him, now parted in a soft instinctive invitation, blind to everything except the fierce excitement scorching and burning through her body as his mouth possessed hers—and she melted beneath the kiss which her traitorous body had been craving.

Weakly winding her arms about his neck, she abandoned herself to the overpowering, deeply sensual need which had so firmly gripped her—a need so intense that, as always, it totally obliterated all thought and all caution. So much so that, trapped in a dense mist of passion and desire as she was, it was some moments before she realised that the loud, imperative ringing in her ears was coming from the telephone behind her.

'Forget it!' he muttered impatiently against her lips as she made a belated attempt to wriggle from his embrace.

But the damage was done. Not only was she shattered to discover that, yet again, she'd been a pathetically weak victim of her own, overriding passion for this man, but, as she soon learned, even allowing him to enter the apartment had been, without a doubt, the gravest mistake she'd ever made in her life.

With his arms tightening about her restless figure like bands of steel, there was nothing Samantha could do as her answering machine clicked into action, and they could both clearly hear her own voice asking the caller to leave a message.

'*Hi, Sam! There's a terrific party going on here in the club tonight!*' Georgie's voice seemed to fill the room. '*Edwina's fed up with me. But I couldn't stand the country—it was like being buried alive—so I rushed back to town. But I wanted to say how thrilled I am to hear that you're expecting a baby! Don't blame Edwina, by the way—I twisted her arm and made her tell me all! So I... Stop it, James, I'm trying to talk to my sister...*' There was a loud clattering noise, accompanied by the heavy thump of hard rock music in the background.

Matt's face was deathly pale beneath his tan, his eyes hard, glittering chips of green ice as he stared down at the girl who, having been frozen still as a statue, suddenly made a frantic, desperate attempt to break free of his embrace and silence the call.

'*Oh, no, you don't!*' he drawled in a dangerously low, menacing voice as she struggled violently in his arms, his iron grip tightening to hold her firmly imprisoned against his chest. 'Because I have a distinct feeling that this is something I *really* ought to hear.'

Almost collapsing with fear and horror at the situation in which she now found herself, there was nothing Samantha could do. There was nowhere to go, nowhere to hide as Georgie, having sorted out her boyfriend, continued to completely wreck her older sister's life.

'*Oops...sorry about that. I must have dropped the phone. Anyway...darling Sam, I hope you're all right. Are you going to marry the baby's father? Because if you do I absolutely insist on being a bridesmaid,*' Georgie prattled artlessly, driving the nails even further into her sister's coffin. '*I was really upset when you refused to let me waltz down the aisle at your wedding to Alan. Still...that's all water under the bridge, isn't it? Anyway...I just wanted to say lots of love and...oh, help!*'

The battery on this mobile phone is running out. I'll have to go, darling. Byeee!'

If the wooden floor beneath her shaking legs had suddenly collapsed and she'd been able to fall down into oblivion, Samantha would more than willingly have done so. Unfortunately, there was nothing she could do but stand frozen in limbo, her eyes clamped tightly shut as she waited for the storm to break over her head.

CHAPTER NINE

SHAKING with fear in anticipation of a quite dreadful, horrendous scene, Samantha was shocked to find herself being suddenly lifted off her feet, carried swiftly through to her bedroom, before being lowered slowly and carefully down on to her bed.

'I'm not going to insult either of us by asking whether the baby is mine—because, of course, it must be.'

Matt's voice sounded amazingly calm and composed, his words seeming to echo strangely in her ears as she lay exhausted against the pillows, still not daring to open her eyes.

'When is the baby due?' he asked quietly, sitting down on the bed beside her.

'January,' she whispered.

'So it was in New York that you conceived the baby?'

She nodded, a weak tear escaping from beneath her tightly clenched eyelids and rolling slowly down her face. 'That first time we made love. After dinner at the Four Seasons. We didn't…it all happened so quickly. I'm sorry, Matt.' She gave a helpless shrug, forcing herself to open her eyes and gaze weepily up at him. 'I guess it's just one of those things…'

'Shush…' he murmured, whipping a large white handkerchief from the top pocket of his jacket and gently wiping her face.

'I'm not saying it isn't all a bit of a shock,' he admitted, a slight flush on his high cheekbones as he gave a low rumble of faintly embarrassed laughter. 'However, it's clearly no good crying over spilt milk. You're expecting my baby—and we must simply decide what we're going to do about it—right?'

Not waiting for her reply, he rose from the bed and began pacing slowly up and down the room.

'We've got quite a lot of time in hand before the baby's born. So, there's clearly no need to panic. However, there are one or two things we must get sorted out straight away. We have to arrange to get married—which means obtaining a licence from somewhere, I presume? Although I imagine your older sister, Edwina, would be able to help you with those sort of arrangements?'

'Just a minute...' she mumbled, struggling to sit up on the bed. She was still feeling stunned by the speed of events. Not to mention her total astonishment at Matt's cool, calm acceptance of the fact that she was expecting his baby.

'There won't be any time for a honeymoon, of course, because I'm far too busy at the moment.' He turned to flash her a quick smile before continuing to tick the items off on his fingers. 'However, it's going to be important to book you into a good hospital for the birth...'

'Hang on!' she said as the confusion and bewilderment at the speed of events gradually cleared from her mind. 'There are still a lot of things we have to talk about.'

'I'm assuming that you've already got a good doctor,' he added, completely ignoring her muttered protest. 'However, we ought to take advice from another top medical opinion, just to be on the safe side.'

Not at all happy about the way Matt seemed to be suddenly taking charge of her life, Samantha tried several times to halt the flow. But, as he continued to walk up and down in front of the bed, making sweeping decisions and arrangements for both herself and also her baby, she decided that she'd just have to wait until he ran out of steam. Because there was obviously a lot more at stake between her and Matt than her unplanned pregnancy.

'In fact, the more I think about it,' he was saying, 'I

think a country wedding—maybe in your sister's local village church?—would be perfect at this time of year.'

And then, clearly struck by a sudden thought, he spun around on his heel to stare down at her.

'I think the news that I'm about to be a father must have gone to my head,' he said slowly. 'Because there is something else, isn't there? That crazy younger sister of yours, Georgie, made some reference to the fact that you'd been married before—right?'

Samantha gave a heavy sigh. 'Yes...' she nodded. 'Yes, I'm afraid so.'

'But you are divorced?' he probed, coming to sit down beside her once again.

'God—yes!' She gave a bitter laugh. 'I should never have married Alan in the first place. The marriage only lasted a few months—which is why I haven't said anything about it before now. I...I really didn't want to remind myself of just what an idiot I'd been.'

Matt shrugged his broad shoulders. 'These things happen,' he murmured, adding with a crooked grin, 'However, it's a relief to know that we haven't got to organise a divorce before being able to make arrangements for our wedding!'

'Slow down, Matt. For one thing, I haven't even agreed to this marriage. And for another...'

'Don't be ridiculous!' He waved away her words as if they were totally irrelevant. 'Now, I think you'd better tell me about your first marriage. And then we can forget it ever happened, all right?'

Samantha gave a helpless shrug. She obviously didn't want to go into all the ins and outs of her marriage to Alan. But, since she was carrying Matt's baby, he undoubtedly had a right to know about that unhappy episode in her past.

Taking a quick decision to omit any reference to the motivation which had originally led her to agree to wed Alan Gifford, she merely confined herself to explaining—

although she and her ex-husband were now good friends—exactly why the marriage had only lasted a few months. Just as long as it had taken the two young people to discover that they had absolutely nothing in common.

'Alan hated towns. He wanted to spend his life deep in the country, where he could concentrate on his painting, while I was set on a financial career in the City. He thoroughly disapproved of the buzz I got from closing a financial deal—and I hated the place always being in a mess and smelling of paint and turpentine. On top of which, all his arty friends loathed and despised every one of my business colleagues. Quite honestly, we could hardly agree on the time of day, let alone any serious major decisions. It was a complete and utter disaster!'

'I'm sorry,' Matt murmured. 'But, from what you say, it does seem as though you've managed to remain friends with your ex-husband. That has to count for something, surely?'

She sighed. 'I hope so. I did go through a period of deep depression. But I came to see that just about everyone takes a wrong turning at some point. The great thing is to try and not do it too often,' she added wryly.

'And I guess that brings me fairly neatly to the point at issue,' she continued, swinging her legs off the other side of the bed and walking slowly around it towards her dressing table. 'It isn't nearly such a simple equation—"Samantha's pregnant: ring out the wedding bells"—as you seem to think. I'm not knocking the way you've taken the news...' She turned to give him a wry smile as she pulled out a stool and sat down in front of her dressing-table mirror. 'You've been remarkably kind and considerate about the situation, Matt—far more than I'd ever thought possible. But there are still some major problems which we need to discuss. The fact is...' she swung around to face him once more '...I don't see how your offering to marry me—much as I appreciate your intention of doing "the right thing"—goes anywhere towards solving the differences between us.'

'Oh, no—not that utterly *stupid* business you were going on about earlier this evening? I told you it was absolute *rubbish*!' he grated, rising swiftly to his feet and pacing up and down the floor behind her.

'You really must be totally paranoiac, Sam, to even think I'd do such a thing,' he thundered angrily. 'For one thing, you weren't Minerva's pension fund manger when we first met up, in New York—right? As far as I was aware, you were merely an ordinary member of your department. So, the idea of me being able to seduce an intelligent woman into behaving in a thoroughly unethical, immoral manner—or that you could manage to persuade everyone else in your firm to blindly follow your advice—is clearly absolute *nonsense*!'

Almost gasping, feeling as if she'd just received a hard blow to the solar plexus, Samantha stared blindly at him in the mirror. Was it possible that she'd been hopelessly wrong about him all these weeks? If so, it looked as if she might have made a quite dreadful mistake. But…but that must mean that she really *had* become totally paranoiac, as Matt claimed.

'Quite frankly, Sam, I'm simply not prepared to discuss this subject any further. It's total and utter rubbish. And if you can't see that I can only suggest you'd better make an appointment to visit a psychiatrist!'

'Thank you for those few kind words,' she snapped. 'But even if I was wrong…even if I *did*, perhaps, come to some wrong conclusions—I'm still going to have to give up my job, aren't I?'

'So…?' He stopped his pacing for a moment to stare at her in surprise. 'Yes…yes, I know…' he said as she opened her mouth to utter a heated protest. 'I'm well aware of how much you enjoy your job. You've obviously done very well, and have achieved considerable success. And yes…I can see that under the present circumstances, with you now expecting my baby, things might be a bit awkward for you as head of the pension fund department at Minerva.'

'That's putting it mildly!' she ground out through clenched teeth.

'Relax! It's hardly the end of the world, Sam! In any case, and just between ourselves, this whole take-over business may well be resolved without any blood-letting on either side. Besides, leaving aside any false modesty, you are a well-qualified and highly regarded member of your profession—right?' And when she nodded in confirmation he merely shrugged his shoulders. 'Well, there you are.'

'No. That's the whole point, Matt. I don't know *where* I am any longer.' She gritted her teeth in exasperation. 'You're completely missing the point. There's no way I can remain in my present job when you, I and soon the whole world will know that I'm expecting your baby. It just won't do.'

He brushed an impatient hand through his dark hair. 'No, you're quite right, of course. While both you and I know—only too clearly!—that you're capable of making a decision on the facts, everyone else would come to the conclusion that your judgement was highly suspect.'

'You're quite right, they would,' she agreed with a heavy sigh.

'Well, as I've already said, it's not the end of the world. I'd obviously prefer to have a wife at home looking after my baby. However, there's no reason why, in the fullness of time, you shouldn't get another job in the City. I'm no anti-feminist, Sam, as well you know. And I'd certainly never try to stop you doing anything you really wanted to.'

It was no good. There was no way that he was going to see that this was, for her, a major tragedy. She loved her work, and she'd been so thrilled about her new promotion. But he really didn't think it was important.

Despite playing lip-service to currently politically correct thinking, Matt was obviously a typical member of the male species. His work came first—and hers a very long way afterwards. But that wouldn't matter so much if, at any point in the last hour, he'd made any mention of how he really felt about her.

'The thing is...' She hesitated for a moment while fiddling nervously with the silver-backed hairbrush which had belonged to her Swedish grandmother. 'Even leaving aside the...er...question about my work—about which we clearly don't agree—there's still the question of our...er...personal involvement.'

'Really, Sam—what an idiot you are!' He laughed, coming over to stand behind her, gazing quizzically at her reflection in the mirror as he placed his hands on her shoulders.

'I don't think you can get much *more* personally involved than getting married and having a baby—do you?' he murmured, slowly sliding his hands down over her full breasts and bringing them to rest on her stomach. 'It's been a bit of a shock, of course, but I'm really rather excited by the thought of becoming a father,' he murmured, lowering his head to press a kiss on her neck.

'That's not what I meant,' she murmured breathlessly, her heart rate beginning to race at the touch of his soft lips on her flesh. 'There's a lot more to marriage than pregnancy. I mean...this was just supposed to be a love affair. No...no emotional involvement, et cetera, et cetera. And you've never really been interested in any form of commitment—right?'

'We're going to get married. And if *that* isn't a commitment I don't know what is!' he told her with a short, husky bark of laughter, slowly trailing his hands up over her slim figure. 'I'm pleased about the baby, of course. But I have to say that I'm *far* more thrilled by the prospect of having your lovely body in my bed every single night,' he added thickly, his fingers closing possessively about her full breasts.

Trying to ignore the siren call of his devastating sex appeal, and the sensual touch of his hands on her flesh, Samantha made a desperate attempt to pull herself together.

'Where, exactly, is this…this bed of yours going to be located? In London? New York?'

'What does it matter where we live, as long as we're together, hmm…?' he murmured, before glancing down at his watch and grimacing with annoyance.

'Sorry, sweetheart—I'll have to go. I've got an early breakfast meeting with some important guys at Claridge's. And I've got a whole mass of work to do before then,' he said, quickly straightening up and giving her a peck on the cheek, before walking towards the door.

'Matt, we really do need to talk, and—'

'I'm sorry, darling. But I really do have to go—right now. I realise that you can't take any calls from me at your office.' He turned to give her a wry grin as he walked to the door. 'So, I'll try and contact you here, at home, the first chance I get. However, give me a ring when you've had a good hard think about everything we've discussed tonight. Believe me, there's really no problem.'

'Yes, Matt. I will have a good hard think about everything,' she promised as he opened the bedroom door, swiftly blowing her a kiss before striding quickly through the main room, on his way out of the apartment.

True to her promise, Samantha did think hard and long about all that had passed between them that night.

In fact, the next morning, after phoning to tell Henry that she wouldn't be in the office that day, she did little else during the next twenty-four hours but slowly and methodically review her past and contemplate her future life—with the same degree of intense concentration that she would have brought to bear on a particularly difficult, important decision at work.

At last, after having come to a final, inescapable conclusion based on all the facts available to her, Samantha eventually picked up the telephone.

Matt gave a heavy sigh as he leaned back in his chair. All this zipping back and forth across the Atlantic—despite the comfort and speed of travelling by Concorde—was playing havoc with his sleep patterns.

'OK, Ruth. I guess that just about wraps everything up—for the moment,' he told his personal assistant. 'I know I've been a hard taskmaster these last few weeks. But if you could get that e-mail off to Australia as soon as possible I'd be very grateful,' he added with a charming, if weary smile.

'Hurtling around the globe is not a recipe for good health,' Ruth informed him bluntly.

Having worked in the London office of Broadwood Securities for the past fifteen years, she felt perfectly at liberty to give the company's recently appointed chief executive the benefit of her good advice. 'You'd better try and get a good night's sleep. Quite frankly, Mr Warner, you're looking pretty dreadful.'

Matt laughed. 'Thank you, dear Ruth, for those few kind words! And believe me,' he added with a tired yawn, 'I fully intend to grab some sleep just as soon as I can.'

'Humph!' his assistant snorted in disbelief as she left the room. Her handsome new boss might be a human dynamo, but he was going to have to learn—just like everyone else she'd ever worked for—that you couldn't cram a week's work into twenty-four hours.

His eyes gritty with tiredness, Matt glanced down at his watch. 'Damn!' he muttered, realising that once again he'd missed an opportunity to call Samantha. He had no hope of getting through to her in her office, so he'd just have to wait until later this evening before contacting her at home, in her apartment.

As the afternoon wore on, and he managed to make serious inroads into the large amount of urgent work requiring his attention, Matt was just wondering whether he could chance his arm by taking a few minutes' break for a cold shower in his executive washroom, when one of his bright young aides knocked and entered his office.

'Well, it looks as if we've got some really good news at last!' the young man told him with a wide smile. 'The evening paper has just hit the streets. I think you'll be pleased about a piece in their "City People" report, at the back of the business section. That woman was always going to be a thorn in our flesh. Much too feisty and independent.'

'Hmm...?' Matt murmured, not really paying his aide a great deal of attention as he quickly scanned a fax which had just been received from their Bonn office. 'Who's feisty and independent?'

'You know, that woman I warned you about—Miss...' He glanced down at the newspaper in his hand. 'Miss Samantha Thomas—yeah, that's right.'

'*What?*'

'It's like I said,' his aide said, handing the newspaper to his boss, and pleased to see that he had engaged Mr Warner's full and undivided attention. 'That huge block of shares owned by Minerva was always going to be a problem, right?' he continued cheerfully. 'And, with her appointment as their pension fund manager, there was no saying which way that damned woman would jump. Still, with her resignation, we've now got a completely different ball game, right?'

Completely ignoring the young man, who was busy cracking his knuckles with excitement at the thought of a new and possibly inexperienced appointee to the position at Minerva, Matt quickly jabbed a button on the intercom and called Ruth back into the room.

'When you've sent off that e-mail, and finished any other urgent business which simply cannot wait, I want you to drop everything and concentrate on this...' He scribbled furiously on a piece of paper in front of him. 'Here are some names and addresses. I want the phone numbers of all these people and I want them fast. And once you've got them on the line I want them put through to me on a priority basis. So get on with it, Ruth. And as for you...' He jabbed an angry forefinger at the young man. *'Get out!'*

Left alone in his office, Matt once again swiftly scanned the brief report, obviously based on a press release from Minerva Utilities Management, regretting the sudden resignation, on health grounds, of their recently appointed pension fund manager, Miss Samantha Thomas.

'Health grounds? What *health grounds*?' he grated angrily, before a winking light on the telephone in front of him indicated an outside line. Seizing up the receiver, he gave a sigh of relief as he heard Edwina's calm, cool English voice.

An hour later, he was cursing the entire population of the calm, cool English nation, swearing violently under his breath as he paced up and down the thick carpet of his luxuriously appointed office.

What the hell was going on? Nobody seemed to know where Samantha had got to. Even Edwina had professed not to have any idea why her sister had so suddenly resigned from her job.

In fact, on balance, he'd believed her when she'd told him that she really didn't know where Samantha was. 'I'm sorry, Matt. All I know is that her apartment seems to be empty at the moment, and she's left no forwarding address. I don't know what's been going on between you two...but, whatever it is, she obviously needs help. Please try and find her as soon as possible.'

Having assured her that he would do everything within

his power to trace her sister, Matt was now burning with exasperation at not being able to fulfil his promise.

Pacing up and down, buried in thought, he suddenly stopped and stood quite still for a moment, before clicking his fingers with annoyance at his own stupidity. Swiftly calling his secretary back into the room, he issued another rapid set of instructions.

When Ruth returned, some ten minutes later, he was surprised to note an amused, wry expression on her face as she placed a file on the desk in front of him.

'That was quick!' he murmured.

'The most difficult part of the task you set me was obtaining a list of people employed by Minerva,' she told him with a slight shrug. 'Of course, once I confirmed that a Henry Graham was indeed employed by the firm, the rest was easy.'

'You're a marvel, Ruth!' he breathed thankfully as he opened the file.

'Not really, Mr Warner,' she murmured, her amusement now clearly visible. 'Because the Honourable Henry Graham is the only son and heir of Lord Parker, one of the directors of Minerva Utilities Management, with whom you are at the moment, I believe, involved in some...er...very private discussions.'

Matt stared at her blankly for a moment, before shaking his dark head and laughing ruefully at his own folly.

'I should have worked it out for myself. Unfortunately, it's that damn business of English aristocrats so often having a surname quite different to that of their title,' he said with another bark of wry laughter. 'OK, Ruth. It's now Friday afternoon. So, can you please ring Lady Parker, at their country house in Surrey, and make an urgent appointment for me to see his Lordship—and his son—tomorrow morning? I'm sure I don't have to tell you,' Matt added, 'that I want this call kept strictly under wraps...?'

'You're quite right—you don't!' his personal assistant retorted crushingly, causing her boss to feel as if he was back at school, being told off by a stern headmistress, as she added, 'If you want my opinion, Mr Warner, I would sternly advise you to find your young lady and marry her as soon as possible. That way, we might all be able to get on with the far more serious business of running this company.'

'Yes, Ruth,' he said meekly, his green eyes glinting with amusement as her stern expression relaxed for a moment, and it seemed—although he wasn't *entirely* sure—that she gave him a slight wink of her eyelid before turning to leave the room.

Lord Parker's Elizabethan country mansion was surrounded by luxuriant green pastures, the large park surrounding the house dotted with clumps of ancient oak trees, under which sheep were peacefully grazing.

Having visited this house only last week, Matt couldn't help thinking as he drove his hired car down the long, gravelled drive leading to the house that it was a perfect example of a grand English country seat. In fact, he couldn't really blame Samantha if, instead of what little he had to offer, she had decided to accept the hand, heart and all the future worldly possessions of the Honourable Henry Graham.

However, after being greeted by Henry's father, and escorted to the large, book-lined library, he only took five minutes to realise that Henry—however good-looking he might appear to be—was not a serious threat. There was no way that bright, clever girl Samantha Thomas would have agreed to marry such a charming nincompoop.

'Mr Warner has given me his solemn word that he will not, in any shape or form, discuss the current take-over situation he's facing at the moment,' Lord Parker was telling his son firmly. 'He merely wishes to discuss another, quite private subject with you, Henry, and I have agreed to act as an honest broker, to ensure that the Stock

Exchange rules are not infringed in any way. Do you understand the position?'

'Yeah. Relax, Dad—I'm not *that* stupid,' Henry muttered, waiting until Lord Parker had left the room before informing Matt that his father could be 'really heavy' at times.

'I'm perfectly well aware that you must be here because of Samantha,' the younger man added, sitting himself down in a comfortable chair and regarding his visitor with some interest. 'So, what is it you want to know?'

If Matt had thought that it would be easy to sort out young Henry, he soon had cause to revise his opinion. In fact, he was annoyed at himself for not remembering that, having survived with all their possessions intact for so many hundreds of years, the British aristocracy were an extremely tough, hard-nosed group of people.

Very polite and extremely courteous, Henry listened to everything Matt had to say without betraying, by even the flicker of an eyelid, that he had any interest in the subject. Even when Matt managed, at last, to provoke a reaction, the younger man remained an extremely stubborn, hard nut to crack.

'Well, yeah,' Henry finally admitted with a shrug, having been harshly accused of failing to declare his own romantic interest in Samantha. 'It's no secret that I'm crazy about her.' Henry shrugged again. 'I always have been. Not that she ever looked at me, of course. Sam was always far too tied up in her career to get involved with anybody in the office. Unfortunately, she now has no career—*thanks to you*! So, why should I help you, when all you've done is ruin her life? And you didn't even have the decency to tell the poor girl that you loved her,' Henry added grimly, by now clearly extremely angry with the stranger sitting across the room.

'OK…calm down,' Matthew told him soothingly. 'If you think I'm the sort of guy who'd get someone pregnant and ask her to marry me without being in love with her, then all I can say is you're way off beam. Of course I love the damn girl! Why else do you think I'm rushing around the countryside, trying to find out what's happened to her?'

'Well…from all I can gather, you never actually *said* that you loved her, did you? And it's no good telling *me*,' Henry added with devastating logic. 'It's Sam you should have told, isn't it?'

'Yes, you're quite right,' Matt acknowledged with a heavy sigh, before using every ounce of persuasion at his command in trying to extract Samantha's whereabouts from Henry, who, he was quite convinced, knew exactly where she was to be found. And he said as much to Henry.

'No.' The younger man shook his head. 'You're wrong. Sam had me weighed up right from the time when I first started working for her. She *knows* that I'm not too clever. So, she's bound to have worked out that you'd try to twist my arm—right?'

Matt nodded slowly, acknowledging what such frank honesty must have cost the younger man. 'OK…but I'm still quite sure that you do know *something*,' he said, adding forcefully, 'I'm not leaving here until I've damn well got it out of you!'

Henry sighed. 'All right—I suppose it's male solidarity time,' he said slowly. 'I *don't* know where she is—and that's the honest truth. All I was able to get out of her was the fact that it's somewhere in the English countryside—which means that you can, at least, narrow down your search by ruling out Scotland, Wales and Ireland.'

'And…? Come on!' Matt demanded grimly. 'I *know* there's something else. So spit it out!'

'I could be wrong,' Henry warned him. 'Sam was very upset at the time and had, incidentally, just turned down my *own* proposal of marriage. But she did mutter something, and I quote: "If Matt really loves me, he'll know where to find me." So, you'd better get your thinking cap on, hadn't you?' he added as his father walked into the room.

'I hope you've got everything sorted out,' Lord Parker murmured, before reminding his visitor that they still had some private business to sort out between themselves.

However, as the elderly peer politely stood aside, to allow him to lead the way out of the room, Matt suddenly halted, before turning slowly around to face father and son.

'It could be—providing that I've solved the puzzle correctly—that I may owe young Henry, here, an enormous debt of gratitude,' he said slowly. 'So, it seems only fair and just to tell you, in front of your father—' he smiled briefly at the younger man '—that possibly everyone—including my dear future wife!—has seriously underestimated your capabilities. Because you strike me as having the cardinal virtues of honesty, discretion, loyalty and a tenacity of purpose which is both rare and truly admirable.

'I don't think you'll ever make chairman or managing director of a company, Henry,' he continued thoughtfully. 'But I have no problem in believing, as you grow older and become less frivolous, that you may well eventually attain the number two position of vice-chairman or vice-principal of an organisation.'

'Really?' Henry blinked, his cheeks turning pink with pleasure.

'Oh, yes, I think so. In fact, I'll be pleased to offer you a job in my company any time you please.'

'Well, how about that, Dad?' Henry turned to grin at the stunned expression on his father's face. 'Maybe I'm not *quite* so dim as you thought, after all!'

What a wonderfully hot summer it was, Samantha told herself, putting down her book with a heavy sigh, leaning back against a tussock of grass as she raised her face to gaze up through the dappled shade of the willow tree, to where the hot sun blazed down overhead.

She'd always loved this part of the country. When she'd urgently needed to get out of London, to gain some space—some peace and quiet in which to think through not only the mess she'd already made of her life, but what she was going to do in the future—it was to this deeply rural Oxfordshire village, which held such happy memories, that she'd instinctively turned.

And it had been the right decision. During the past week, she'd been able to take stock of all that had happened to her over the past three months. However, when reviewing her own behaviour, Samantha hadn't spared herself. There was no doubt that she'd made many stupid decisions, and come to some quite wrong conclusions.

But she now had to put all that behind her—and concentrate on the future. A future which didn't just concern herself, alone. It was the baby, to whom she would give birth in under seven months' time, which must now be her foremost priority. And, while it would have been so easy to simply do nothing, to let Matt completely take over and run her life for her, she was now quite certain that she'd made the right decision.

However, resigning from the job she loved, and accepting her chairman's kindly if frank agreement that she was, under the circumstances, making the right decision, had been dreadfully upsetting.

'We're going to miss you, Miss Thomas,' he'd said with a slow shake of his head. 'This whole situation is extremely unfortunate, of course. However, I agree with you that there was only one moral and ethical decision you could take, under these trying circumstances. And you are to be congratulated on acting so promptly in the interests of this firm.'

Pausing for a moment, he'd continued, 'I'd like to say, strictly off the record, that I realise it can't have been easy to come here to see me today. And, when the dust has settled…well, let's just say that if and when you should require a job in the future I will personally guarantee to exert my best efforts on your behalf, amongst my contacts in the City.'

And that really had been very generous of him, Samantha told herself as she began packing away the remains of her picnic lunch. Almost as kind and generous as Henry, she thought with a small, rueful smile, recalling her assistant's amazingly kind and generous offer to make an honest woman of her.

It had been impossible, of course, to keep the truth behind her sudden resignation from Henry. Turning up at her apartment with a heavy box full of her personal books and papers which she'd left in the office, he had adamantly refused to leave without being told the true reason for Samantha's departure from a job she'd loved.

'I'm not being kind or generous!' Henry had exploded when, after admitting the circumstances leading up to her resignation, she'd gently but firmly rejected his offer of marriage.

'I want you, Sam. I always have. And I couldn't care less whose baby it is!' he'd continued firmly. 'It would be *our* child when we married, right? And besides,' he'd added swiftly, 'I know that Ma and Pa would be absolutely delighted that I was settling down, at last. And, of course, money's no problem. I've got more than enough for both of us—and a horde of kids!'

'Oh, Henry…you really are a very sweet, kind man,' she'd murmured. 'And I really do appreciate what you've just said. But it simply wouldn't work, I'm afraid. Not when I'm in love with someone else. And besides,' she'd added, trying to lighten the heavy atmosphere, 'I'd hate to blow your chances with the chairman's daughter!'

'Oh, Sam!' he'd groaned impatiently. 'That was only a passing fancy. It's *you* that I've always been crazy about—and well you know it!'

And it was because she *did* know just how it felt to be

in love with someone who couldn't return her love that
she'd taken a great deal of trouble to let him down gently.
And, yet again, she'd known that it had been the right
decision on her part. Having once made a disastrous
choice by marrying someone for all the wrong reasons,
she'd been quite determined never to repeat the same mistake ever again.

The loud, rhythmic sound of water flowing over the
mill beside the small bridge was definitely having a sop-
orific effect, she thought, leaning back and yawning as
she gave up the struggle to try and keep her eyes open.

The Mill and Old Swan at Minster Lovell had changed
somewhat since she'd last stayed here with Matt, all those
years ago. The six-hundred-year-old country inn now also
provided a conference and training centre for businessmen, as well as ordinary visitors. But sitting here, under
the willow trees on the other side of the river from the
half-timbered old building—and with the noise of passing
traffic completely drowned by the loud sound of fast
gushing water—she felt as though she was quite alone on
a private island.

But she couldn't stay here buried in the country for
ever, of course, Sam told herself, feeling too tired and
weary after yet another sleepless night to come to any
firm decision about her future. She had wondered if it
might be a good idea to turn her back on the City of
London, and maybe take up a job teaching economics, at
a college of further education. But she could afford to
wait until the posts were advertised, later on in the summer, before having to make that decision.

Because it was becoming clear that she was going to
need as much time as possible to get her act together, and
get over her overwhelmingly strong feelings for Matt.
During the past few days, there'd been no lessening of
her intense longing for him, or the aching need for the
caress of his hands on her body; her nights had been
haunted by his powerful, charismatic presence, as his dark

shadow stalked arrogantly and forcefully through her restless and troubled sleep.

She could only hope that old cliché—time is a great healer—would eventually prove to be true. But she feared it would take a very long time, if ever, for her to finally eliminate him from her head and her heart. In the meantime, she must just concentrate on making a decision about whether to go for that teaching job. If only…if only she didn't feel *quite* so tired…

How long she'd been asleep in the warm sunshine, Samantha had no idea. But, eventually becoming aware of something—an insect or a blade of grass?—tickling her cheek, she raised a sleepy hand to brush it away. Unfortunately, her actions didn't seem to have any effect and, as the heavy mists in her brain gradually dispersed, she slowly opened her eyelids.

A second later, she had clamped them tightly shut again, her slim figure suddenly becoming tense and rigid with shock.

Oh, Lord! She was hallucinating! She must have finally lost her mind…totally flipped! Obviously, the strain of the last week had proved too much for her to cope with. Because…for one dreadful moment…she could have sworn that it was Matt's tall figure lying beside her on the river bank. And that…that just wasn't *possible*!

Once again, she could feel the piece of grass brushing gently against her cheek. Only this time it was accompanied by a low rumble of laughter, coming from beside her left ear. The sick, sudden apprehensive lurch of her stomach left her feeling as if she was in an elevator, hurtling down from an enormous height, as she forced herself to open her eyes. Slowly…very slowly and cautiously, she turned her head.

Oh, my God! It really *was* Matt, lying beside her on the grass, his arm, bent at the elbow, propping up his dark head as he smiled down into her utterly shocked, stunned blue eyes.

CHAPTER TEN

IT MUST have been the sudden shock. Why else would a grown-up, sophisticated woman of nearly thirty years of age react to the totally unexpected appearance of her lover by suddenly bursting into a storm of tears?

'Oh, Matt...!' she sniffed as he gently dried her eyes with yet another of his large white handkerchiefs. 'I'm s-sorry to be behaving like an absolute fool. I'm not normally the sort of person who weeps all over the place. I really...'

'It's all right, sweetheart,' he murmured, gently stroking the back of the girl cradled in his arms, her head now buried in the curve of his broad shoulder. 'I know that "strong men don't cry" and all that sort of thing. But I'm not ashamed to admit that I shed a tear or two when I feared that I'd lost you for ever.'

'I'm sorry. I had to get away. I just couldn't cope with everything, and...' She gave a muffled, heavy sigh.

'And you believed that I didn't love you? How *could* you have been such an idiot? Surely you must know that I've *always* been crazy about you. Ever since I laid eyes on a slim, beautiful young girl attending one of my lectures, the sun from a window high in the wall streaming down to highlight her thick, shimmering cloud of white-gold hair. I was lost...right from that first moment! Why else would I have taken such an enormous gamble? Or be prepared to face the very real risk of losing my university appointment?'

'Yes, but...but "love" seems to mean different things to different people, doesn't it?' she said, slowly raising her head to gaze steadily up into his eyes.

'You said you loved me, Matt, all those years ago—
but look what happened to us. And yes,' she added
quickly, 'I do now understand exactly *why* you acted as
you did. But, if you could take such a ruthless action
once, it seemed likely that you could do so again. And I
was *not* prepared to go into a hurriedly arranged marriage
with the father of my baby, when he might well repeat
his actions of nine years ago.'

She gave an unhappy shrug of her shoulders. 'Besides
which, you made it quite clear in New York that you were
only interested in an affair. Just sex. No emotional nonsense…no commitment. And the fact that you were now
prepared to act like a gentleman, and "do the right thing"
by myself and the baby, didn't seem to alter the basic
fact that, without true love on both sides, our marriage
hadn't a hope of lasting more than a year or two, if that.'

'Oh, my sweet, darling idiot!' He sighed heavily. 'I
sometimes wonder if men and women inhabit the same
planet! When a man tells you that he's *absolutely crazy*
about you, believe me, he's in love! OK, OK…' Matt
added hurriedly as she stirred restlessly in his arms. 'I
take your point about the different meanings of the word
"love". But cutting you out of my life, all those years
ago, was the hardest decision I've ever had to take. It
took me years to recover from the pain. And it's probably
the reason why I could never bring myself—when it came
to the crunch—to make a firm commitment to any other
woman.'

'Yes, but in New York you said that you just wanted
a love affair, and—'

'Oh, come on, Sam! There I was, by the mere chance
of fate, meeting once again the only true love of my life—
right? And discovering, like a clap of thunder, that I was
still as much in love with you as ever. To tell you the
truth, I'd have said *anything*—anything at all—to try and
hang on to you, and somehow prevent you from disap-
pearing out of my life before we'd had a chance to con-

solidate our new relationship,' he admitted with a rueful, slightly embarrassed laugh.

'So, when it quickly became obvious that our love-making was even more glorious than ever, I had to swiftly try and persuade you to agree to having a relationship—which would leave you feeling as free as a bird, but one whereby I saw as much of you as possible. Until such time as I could persuade you to give me another chance.'

'Oh, Matt...if *only* you'd told me the truth, straight away,' she murmured with a heavy sigh.

'How could I? I mean...' he brushed a hand roughly through his dark hair '...for all I knew, you could have had a live-in lover back in London—right? And, God knows, I had to press really hard before you agreed to take me to your sister's for the weekend. Believe me, trying to maintain a long-distance love affair is the absolute pits!'

'Tell me about it!' she muttered feelingly.

'And then...' He gave a heavy sigh. 'And then, in the midst of my new-found euphoria, you landed the promotion of your dreams. Which, unfortunately, soon proved to be *my* worst nightmare come true. I quickly realised that I must contact you as little as possible, keeping my distance, if only for professional reasons. Which you, of course, quickly interpreted as a loss of interest on my part. However, I did all I could to try and talk things through with you. But by then it was all far too late. You were into total paranoia, while I was up to my eyeballs in the take-over. And our wonderful, *wonderful* love affair had become a total snake-pit of emotional confusion!'

'As soon as I learned I was expecting a baby, I knew that I'd eventually have to leave my job,' she admitted with a tremulous sigh. 'Maybe...maybe that was why I clung on so long to the idea that you were double-crossing me. Because, if our affair was over, I *would* have been able to continue working at Minerva. But once you found out about the baby...' she heaved another heavy sigh '...I didn't have any choice but to resign.'

'I know, darling. And I'm truly very sorry about your job. I do realise *just* how much it meant to you. But I've done a lot of thinking over the past week. And now that there's going to be no take-over I really think...'

'What on earth are you talking about?' she demanded. She was subsequently amazed to hear that while she'd been buried deep in the country, and not bothering to read any newspapers, Matt—using Henry's father as a go-between—had negotiated a merger between the two companies.

'You are now looking at the new managing director of Broadwood, Kendal & Laval,' he informed her with a grin, before explaining that everyone, including the Stock Market, was extremely happy about the result, which clearly made a great deal of sense. 'The new headquarters of the company will be in London, where I will now spend most of my time, although I will have to visit New York fairly frequently, of course. I thought of buying a large house in Holland Park, and—'

'*Hang on!*' she suddenly gasped, staring up at him in dawning horror. 'I've just realised that if there's now going to be no take-over there was no need for me to resign from my job!'

'I'm sorry to say that you're quite right,' he told her. But, as Samantha took a deep breath, clearly about to hurl curses of dire retribution down on his dark head, Matt swiftly explained that he'd already been in touch with her chairman, who was prepared to let her resume her old position, if she so wished, after the birth of her baby.

'I don't believe it!' she retorted grimly. 'Why on earth should he put himself out for me? Besides, life is far too fast, too cut-throat in the City. Now I've resigned from the firm, I'd never be given the opportunity to work for them again,' she added gloomily. 'Absolutely no chance!'

'Well, sweetheart—that's where you're completely

wrong!' Matt grinned down at her with amusement, before explaining that both her chairman and Lord Parker had been instrumental in arranging the merger—which they'd seen as the best policy for the pension funds they looked after.

'So, your chairman and I had a long talk. Not only is he *very* happy with the merger, of course, but he has agreed to regard your resignation as coming under the heading of maternity leave. So, if you wish, you may return to your office after the birth of your baby, with no loss of salary or seniority.'

Samantha stared up at him for some time in silence. 'You're not particularly happy about that solution, are you?' she said at last.

'No, not really,' he admitted slowly. 'I wouldn't be honest if I didn't say I'd prefer you to be at home, looking after our children. But if the only way I can persuade you to marry me is to accept that you really *need* the challenge of work—then I'm willing to go along with whatever action you decide to take.'

He hesitated for a moment, before taking a deep breath. 'I love you, Samantha. I've always loved you—and I guess I always will,' he said quietly. 'I want you to marry me. To be the mother of my children, and for us to live in love and harmony for the rest of our days.'

'Oh, *Matt*...!' she whispered as the tears began trickling down her face again.

'Does that mean yes or no?' he demanded, staring down at her, his face suddenly becoming pale and strained. 'Because, if you're going to put me through the hoops by running away again, I'll...I'll... *Oh, God, sweetheart*—I don't know *what* I'll do without you!' he ground out huskily, clasping her tightly to his hard, firm chest.

'I *knew* there was something...' she muttered. 'I mean, how on earth did you manage to find me so quickly?'

He grinned. 'I owe it all to Henry Graham! Yes, I know

you don't think very highly of his brain power. But he was quite astute enough to recall your statement to the effect that, if I *really* loved you, I would know where to find you. And, since I do most truly love, honour and adore you, I knew *just* where to look, didn't I? Where else but the one place where we had been so supremely happy all those years ago?'

Once again, Samantha was privately appalled to discover that, despite thinking of herself as a sophisticated woman, she could be so easily reduced to weeping with untold joy and happiness.

'Come on, Sam!' he demanded urgently. 'Dry those eyes—and put me out of my misery. Because I'm *still* waiting to hear if you're going to marry me.'

'You've been far more kind and generous than I deserve,' she murmured, smiling up at him through her tears. 'And...and both the baby and I—after a *very* brief consultation—are extremely happy to accept the take-over which you've just proposed!'

He laughed. 'My dearest sweetheart—I *really* don't want to hear anything more about take-overs! What *we're* talking about is a Merger—right?'

'Absolutely right!' she agreed with a happy sigh as Matt lowered his head, possessing her lips in a kiss of deep intensity, and total commitment.

Just over six months later, Samantha lay back on the pillows gazing sleepily around the remarkably luxurious, private suite of rooms in a London Hospital.

Sighing with contentment, she lowered her head to smile at the tiny baby lying securely wrapped in her arms. With a fine crop of fluffy, dark hair, her son was already looking remarkably like Matt; the only legacy from his mother seemed to be the bright sapphire-blue eyes, now hidden by his drowsy eyelids as he lay sleepily content and replete at her breast.

No one, least of all herself, could pretend that the actual

process of giving birth was exactly a picnic. But all the pain and discomfort seemed totally unimportant now that she was holding such a precious new life in her arms.

Although she wasn't at all sure that his father had viewed the birth of his son in *exactly* that same light!

Raising her head, she grinned over at the figure of her darling husband, lying stretched out in a large, comfortable chair on the other side of the room. Poor Matt! He was leaning back with his eyes shut, his face pale and drained, and it definitely looked as if she was going to recover from the trauma of childbirth far more quickly than the baby's father!

'Of course I'm going to be there,' he'd told her firmly, when she'd wondered whether he wished to be present at the birth of their child. 'I haven't got any time for those "Childbirth for Men" classes—which strike me as complete nonsense,' he'd added dismissively. 'However, I'm definitely going to be there to see my son being born.'

'Honestly, Matt! You've simply got to face the fact that this baby could well be a *girl*,' Samantha had said, turning to grin at him while cooking supper in their new large home in Holland Park.

She still hadn't decided whether she really would want to go back to work after the baby's birth. Matt's strong recommendation that she ought to wait and see how she felt about leaving her baby in another woman's care made perfect sense. Besides, she was, to her complete surprise, thoroughly enjoying the novelty of being at home every day. In fact, the prospect of going off to the office was becoming less and less attractive.

'We decided not to find out, in advance, whether we're having a boy or a girl,' she'd reminded him sternly, waving a wooden spoon in front of his face. 'And I don't want any sex discrimination in this house!'

'I will, of course, be equally happy if the child turns out to be a girl,' Matt had assured her with a grin. 'However, I wouldn't dream of letting you go through the experience of childbirth without being there by your side.'

Fine words, indeed! Samantha smiled, recalling the events of only a few hours ago.

It was, perhaps, unfortunate that he'd refused to become involved in a 'teach-in' about the birth process. Because, as poor Matt had stood masked and gowned in the delivery room, no one had had time to notice that his tall figure was slowly beginning to sway, his face becoming first pale and then chalky-white, before he'd suddenly slumped to the floor in a dead faint—just as she was about to give birth to their baby.

'*For heaven's sake!*' she'd gasped, unable to stop herself from giggling at the sight of the fearsome business tycoon lying on the floor, with the doctors and nurses all rushing to his side.

'Hang on—*I'm* supposed to be the patient around here!' she'd protested as Matt's tall, handsome figure had been carted out of the delivery room on a stretcher. And, despite the pain and high discomfort, she'd still been smiling at the whole ridiculous situation when she'd finally given birth to their baby son.

How are the mighty fallen! she thought, smiling mistily over at her dear, most beloved husband. He would soon recover, of course, and become his normal, tough self. But she would always treasure that one, highly unusual sight of such a strong, arrogant man being brought to his knees. Totally humbled by the sight of a miracle which took place every minute around the globe: that of a woman bringing new life into this world.

'Are you feeling all right, sweetheart?' he said now, rising slowly from the chair and going through into the *en-suite* bathroom to splash cold water over his face. 'I reckon I made a bit of a fool of myself,' he murmured, walking back into the large room and grinning at her over the top of the towel as he continued to dry his face. 'I really had no idea...'

'It's all right, darling. My lips are sealed!' She smiled. 'Your secret is quite safe with me. God forbid that anyone should learn the terrible truth: that Matthew Warner, feared the length and breadth of the City of London—not to say Wall Street!—should have actually fainted dead away when...'

'OK, OK!' He laughed as he came to sit down on the bed beside her. 'Now, I think it's time to completely change the subject, *if* you don't mind. Because we have to discuss something very important. Which is: what name are we going to give my wonderful new son?'

'Well...' she murmured as he stretched forth a long, tanned finger to stroke the soft, downy skin of the baby's face gently. 'I've been thinking about that. I wondered whether Alexander might not be a rather good name? You know...Alexander the Great, and all that sort of thing?'

'Mmm...I like the sound of that,' he agreed. 'Alexander Warner sounds fine to me. And we'll obviously call him Alex for short, right?'

She nodded happily. 'Alex it shall be. Oh, by the way, have you told Edwina the good news?'

'I haven't had a chance to talk to anyone,' he admitted sheepishly, clearly not feeling entirely back to his old self. 'But apparently she rang up just after you'd given birth to Alex, and sends much love. However, I do have a piece of news.' He grinned. 'Although I'm not at all sure whether it will make you laugh or cry.'

'What news?' she murmured, her heart turning over with joy and happiness as she watched Matt gently removing the baby from her arms, before carefully holding his son cradled against his chest.

'Well, Edwina rang, catching me just as I was about to leave the office to join you here for the birth,' Matt explained. 'Apparently, Georgie has become engaged to be married.'

'Really?' Samantha grinned. 'And which one of her many boyfriends is she going to marry?'

Matt gave a low chuckle of laughter. 'You're never going to believe this, but do you remember how well she and your assistant, Henry Graham, were getting on at our wedding?'

'You don't mean…? But…but they are both as daft as a brush! It will never, never work—not in a month of Sundays!'

'As you know, I think you've always been too hard on Henry. And I happen to think that they *will* be very happy. And, let's face it, at least Georgie is not going to worry about his lack of brains—since she has virtually none herself!'

'I think that's just a *bit* mean,' Samantha protested half-heartedly, feeling she must stand up for her younger sister, however much she agreed with Matt's diagnosis.

'Well, Edwina informs me that Henry's parents are absolutely delighted to know that he's settling down, at last. And Georgie is over the moon at the prospect of being, in the fullness of time, a real ''Lady''!'

Samantha sighed. 'Well, I hope they'll be very happy,' she murmured, suddenly feeling very tired.

'I'm sure they will,' Matt said, placing the baby carefully back in his mother's arms, before deciding to take advantage of the private hospital's comfortable facilities by lying down on the bed beside his beloved wife.

'However,' he added with a tired yawn, 'I reckon there's no way they could *possibly* be any happier than you and I—right?'

'*Absolutely right!*' she murmured softly, and all three members of the Warner family drifted slowly and contentedly off to sleep.

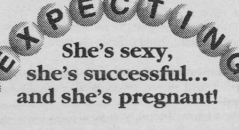

EXPECTING

She's sexy, she's successful... and she's pregnant!

Relax and enjoy these new stories about spirited women and gorgeous men, whose passion results in pregnancies... sometimes unexpectedly! All the new parents-to-be will discover that the business of making babies brings with it the most special love of all....

Harlequin Presents® brings you one **EXPECTING!** book each month throughout 1999. Look out for:

The Unexpected Father by Kathryn Ross
Harlequin Presents® #2022, April 1999

The Playboy's Baby by Mary Lyons
Harlequin Presents® #2028, May 1999

Accidental Baby by Kim Lawrence
Harlequin Presents® #2034, June 1999

Available wherever Harlequin books are sold.

HARLEQUIN®
Makes any time special ™

If you enjoyed what you just read,
then we've got an offer you can't resist!

Take 2 bestselling love stories FREE!

Plus get a FREE surprise gift!

HARLEQUIN PRESENTS®

Wedded Bliss

Penny Jordan Carole Mortimer

Two brand-new stories—for the price of one!—
in one easy-to-read volume.
Especially written by your favorite authors!

Wedded Bliss
Harlequin Presents #2031, June 1999
THEY'RE WED AGAIN!
by Penny Jordan
and
THE MAN SHE'LL MARRY
by Carole Mortimer

There's nothing more exciting than a wedding!
Share the excitement as two couples make their very
different journeys which will take them up the aisle to
embark upon a life of happiness!

Available **next month** wherever Harlequin books
are sold.

HARLEQUIN®
Makes any time special ™

Look us up on-line at: http://www.romance.net

HP2IN1

Coming Next Month

HARLEQUIN PRESENTS®

THE BEST HAS JUST GOTTEN BETTER!

#2031 WEDDED BLISS Penny Jordan & Carole Mortimer
Two complete stories in one book to celebrate Harlequin's
50th anniversary.

THEY'RE WED AGAIN! Penny Jordan
Belle Crawford found herself seated next to her ex-husband
Luc at a wedding. They'd been divorced for seven years so
everyone expected fireworks—and there were...fireworks
sparked by passion!

THE MAN SHE'LL MARRY Carole Mortimer
Merry Baker had been cruelly jilted by the father of her child
eighteen years ago, so she'd never really considered men or
marriage. But after meeting handsome Zack Kingston she had
to change her mind....

#2032 HER GUILTY SECRET Anne Mather
Alex's life had fallen apart when his wife died, and he'd lost
custody of his baby daughter. Now he was suspicious of his
gorgeous new employee, Kate Hughes. Was she involved with
his fight to get his daughter back?

#2033 THE PRICE OF A BRIDE Michelle Reid
Mia agreed to marry millionaire Alexander Doumas so that
both he and her father would gain from the deal. But how
could Mia's real reason for marrying Alex be kept a secret
when she shared such passion with him every night?

#2034 ACCIDENTAL BABY Kim Lawrence
To Jo, gorgeous Liam Rafferty was simply her best friend.
Until one night they accidentally got too close—and Jo
found herself pregnant! Unexpectedly, Liam insisted on
marriage....

#2035 THE GROOM'S REVENGE Kate Walker
India had been about to say "I do" when Aidan, the fiancé
she loved and desired, accused her of being a gold digger
and promptly jilted her. Now Aidan was back wanting
revenge: he'd help India's family, but for a price—India....

#2036 SLEEPING WITH THE BOSS Cathy Williams
Victor Temple worked with his assistant Alice, all day, every
day. Their relationship had always been strictly business—
until now. Suddenly Victor had seen behind her neat
professional disguise and found the real, passionate Alice....